Excerpts from the reviews of:

THE WITCH'S LOST LOVE

"An exciting page-turner."

"This novel had me on the edge of my seat from start to finish."

"Kept me guessing until the end…fun reading, with some surprising twists."

"The information on the Wiccan religion is surprisingly interesting."

"I enjoyed all of the characters and found myself wanting to be a part of Stephanie's nurturing women's Wiccan Circle."

Also by Cathy A. Corn:

BLUE MOON OVER MADAGASCAR
Lilith & the Faeries #1

SMELL THE PLUMERIAS
Lilith & the Faeries #2

FAERY: THE FINAL FRONTIER
Lilith & the Faeries #3

BEYOND THE FAERY PORTAL
Lilith & the Faeries #4

MURDER THROUGH THE LOOKING-GLASS

WRITE YOUR BOOK FOR A MORE AMAZING LIFE

The Witch's Lost Love

CATHY A. CORN

THE WITCH'S LOST LOVE

For information contact **www.CathyACorn.com**.

And don't forget to go outside and gaze at the full moon.

Book interior by Cathy Corn
Cover by GetCovers

First Edition: January 2020

For Isis,

The Women's' Spirituality Circle,

and all who love the earth and her creatures.

And for Anna the cat,

who appeared on our doorstep

and filled our lives with love.

As a general rule, the people with whom we have our strongest emotional ties were usually connected to us in some form in a past life. Souls who are closely related in one lifetime often meet in others.

From *Uncover Your Past Lives* by Ted Andrews

FREE BOOK

FOR JOINING CATHY'S EMAIL LIST

Get a free book of stories for joining Cathy's VIP mailing list
(exclusive updates about new releases,
giveaways, and FREE eBooks).

Sign up at **www.CathyACorn.com.**

Chapter 1

Flames engulfed me, red hot and searing, shooting high into the night sky. Screams of pain and fear surrounded me, yet here I stood bound by ropes and isolated in this spot of destruction. The smell reached my nostrils, acrid and surreal, yet I waited in detachment for the end. Calmness filled my entire being, which extended far beyond the ropes and wooden stake. I heard myself call out with joy, "Goddess, I'm coming! Take me home!"

"You all right, Steph?" I heard beside me. Isis squeezed my hand and I focused in on her face. I felt dizzy and spaced out, the way I did after a vision. I must have been having a vision.

"What happened?" I asked, feeling detached and calm as I had in the flashback, as if being burned at the stake happened every day.

"You called out to the Goddess, Stephanie Gray. Right after you turned pale and stared into the bonfire like a zombie and didn't answer me. It lasted a few minutes, but you scared me. You looked possessed."

My friend Deborah, who called herself Isis, sat beside me in our circle, her face crinkled with concern. Our bonfire crackled, casting light on the faces of the dozen women surrounding it. I inhaled deeply of its pleasant smoke and watched the blue and yellow flames dance a sultry number, a welcome contrast to the roaring, devouring fire in my waking dream.

Maybe our bonfire had somehow triggered the awful scene. I hurried to explain my condition, for our ritual would begin momentarily.

"It was a vision. They started after I joined this group. I've had five flashbacks now about some lifetime hundreds of years ago. I practiced healing work then, just like now."

"That's pretty wild, Moonbeam. Maybe wilder than me. Let's talk after the ritual," she said and rose so that her spider earrings swung in arcs beneath the blonde hair confined in a French braid. She straightened the black sheath dress with cobweb patterns on it and readjusted the purple velvet ground-length cape.

"Welcome, ladies, to the Women's Healing Circle for our Samhain ritual. Though many know this as Halloween, we who practice the old ways celebrate this night when those in spirit are closest and can best communicate with us. Have you all brought pictures of beloved people and pets in spirit? Please place your photos on the altar, of those who have died but live on in our hearts and memories, and in spirit."

Most of us placed items on the rough brown burlap cloth beside our circle. I kissed a photo of my little dog Lady who had died several years ago, then placed it between the orange candles burning above their holders. I examined the pictures of dogs, cats, and people, a dog collar and cat toy. A feather in a plastic container might have come from a parakeet. The animal offerings outnumbered the people offerings two to one.

The fire toasted our fronts, though the chilly night skulked about our backs, nipping at our necks. As Isis led a meditation, I gazed about the surroundings, always happy out in nature. I'd recovered from my disorientation from the vision.

Tall, twisted oaks rose all around us, dark as the night, clinging tightly to dead leaves that rattled with the rare breeze. This remote picnic grove at the far edge of North Park provided perfect secrecy for our ritual. Privacy worked best since our rites had been misunderstood in the past. High above all rode a golden moon still nearly full, promising abundance to make our hopes and dreams appear. A magical moon.

I stared into the fire-lit faces, many Celtic in looks, all expectant as they shifted their long skirts to get comfortable on their thin, padded cushions. We could have been a group in Ireland from hundreds of years ago instead of Pittsburgh ladies, city witches.

We rose and called upon the directions and the elements in unison, our arms outstretched to the sky, constructing our magical circle of power. When we sat back down to sing a song, Isis leaned over to me and whispered, again using my magical name, "Stick around after the ritual, Moonbeam. Got to hear about your vision, plus there's an important item to run by you. An urgent matter."

I raised my eyebrows, then nodded. I'd been coming to Circle six months now, after meeting Isis at a yoga workshop. Somehow, learning about magical healing and meeting with these earnest women gave meaning to my life. I felt closer to the earth and her creatures and ultimately to myself and who I was, which was still a big mystery.

When our ritual finished, the ladies stayed briefly for refreshments, hugging their jackets above their long skirts and dresses. I glanced down at my jeans and jean jacket which looked dull and non-magical. Maybe I'd remember to visit Goodwill this month for more appropriate gear.

After the last lady hugged us good night and left, Isis asked me about my vision. "You were way out there somewhere," she said.

"I never used to have these visions. Now scenes of some past life play like a movie in my head when I'm awake. It's odd; it's too strange." I explained my burning at the stake vision to her.

Isis stared at me, and her jaw dropped open. I heard our bonfire crackling and popping during the brief silence.

"Burned as witches," she finally said, her hand on my arm. "You and I during the Burning Times hundreds of years ago. Even as a kid, Suzie next door set my hair on fire by accident, and it felt natural to be in flames.

"Maybe you see these glimpses because you've returned to the old ways. Or maybe it's a warning." Isis gathered her belongings into a large canvas bag.

That's when the little gnawing sensation started in my upper chest, extending to my throat.

"If it's a warning, I'll pay attention, but I'm staying with Circle. These ladies have been good for me. Maybe I'll give up my rootless existence." Not really rootless any more, for I'd settled down since a fuzzy cat named Tricksie pounced into my life. My transformation included a home and a steady job waitressing. Before that, I'd drifted from job to job—most at minimum wage—and from relationship to relationship. I hadn't played the dating game for several years now. In the past, I'd settled for a lot less than what I wanted in most areas of my life, an underachiever with a capital "U."

"Thought you'd told me you came for the refreshments." Isis teased in the dark. "No, really, you belong with us. I've always thought that."

"Thanks, dear, you know how serious I am. By the way, the cookies tonight were great. Must have gone through a dozen including the ones I stashed in my purse." I winked. "You wanted to tell me something?"

Her voice sounded tired. "It's Flo. She hasn't come to Circle in weeks. I've called her, sent postcards, and still no word."

"Why worry about that?" I asked. "She's probably busy.
Women come and go in this group."

"Something is radically wrong. Flo never stops coming, and there's this strong feeling of danger. Maybe even foul play."

"Shall I help you investigate, Sherlock?" I asked.

"Please, Stephanie. I'm dead serious," Isis said. By the light of the bonfire, I could see her earnest expression. "I fear for her life."

"Surely not. Not Flo."

"It happened before, hundreds of years ago. In my dreams, I see us as healers and wise women, but we were persecuted." Isis pulled her warm cloak tight around her trim figure as if to keep out the past.

I waited for her to continue.

"We helped others and ourselves, and we were burned. We were torched alive, just like in your vision." Her eyes opened wide, and I caught the feeling of her words. This wasn't just a story in a book; this happened to us and other innocent victims.

"But that was way back then. This is now, hundreds of years later," I said, for she seemed a long way off. "Surely in this day and age we need not fear old memories."

"Some things never change. The light has always attracted the darkness. And I believe we who practice our old ways are still in mortal danger. And there's the scapegoat factor," she said in a matter-of-fact tone.

"I'm not sure what you mean, except that we were scapegoats back then."

"I believe history repeats itself. That pattern was passed down over the centuries. I've seen it in my own life. Haven't you ever felt like an innocent victim, like evil turned against you?"

"Yes, on rare occasions," I said, surprised at this twist in our conversation and amazed at her insight. "Maybe it's written into our DNA. I'd like a scientific explanation for all this. It's unpleasant."

"We need to move beyond this pattern, especially now that's there some new menace. Flo didn't quit, not of her own will."

"I'll help you and we'll track her down. But I'm sure she's all right. She got busy with other things."

Isis only smiled as we prepared to leave. A chilly wind kicked up, blowing hair in my face. I buttoned up my jacket.

The golden moon had turned silver now, and the bonfire had dwindled. We would have to kill the remains before we left—park regulations and common sense.

I wondered about Flo as we threw water on the red glowing embers. Steam erupted upward and hissed like faced-off Halloween cats. The power and tenacity of the fire's terminal stages impressed me.

"She didn't give up without a struggle, if I know Flo," Isis said.

"You have strong feelings about this. You seem so sure."

"I'm usually right. Wish I weren't this time. Someone may soon extinguish Flo, just as we put out this fire. Snuff her right out. She's eccentric, but doesn't deserve this."

"It's odd. Our meetings are brighter and more upbeat without her. She had a way of lowering everybody's spirits. She was always whining about one thing or another."

"Are you hiding her somewhere?" Isis asked with laughter in her voice.

"I'd have tried some other approach first, maybe given her cookies laced with herbs to improve her disposition. I always sat on the opposite side of the room from her. Worked great."

"She was like a little warty toad, the kind movie witches use in their potions, except we don't make potions. Maybe an overweight warty toad."

I laughed as we moved toward our cars.

"She would have spoiled the potion. Anyone taking it would be overcome by an urge to whine and complain."

"Maybe we can work on this next week," Isis said. "We'll do what we can for her."

"Do you think the rest of us are in danger?" I was leaning on my car.

"Not yet. But ultimately, yes. I think all of us will eventually be involved in what's happening. And if we stick together and work on this, our chances are much better. A solitary girl might not have a chance."

"Good night, Isis. I'll be talking to you."

"Good night. Thanks for coming."

The moon beckoned from above, more interesting than the park scenery as I drove away. I felt connected to it, not only by my magical name, Moonbeam, but by my very center. The moon and I were one that night.

The talk about Flo didn't concern me as I sailed along the roads toward home. I usually believed Isis, but this time she was imagining things. We were just urban witches involved in jobs, family, and home. Our practice consisted of rituals, using magical methods like aromatherapy, stones, and herbs, and honoring ourselves and the Goddess. Why would anyone bother us, even whiny old Flo? I didn't think so.

I remembered my vision and felt humbled. Certainly strange forces worked beneath the surface of our lives. When a cloud sailed across the moon, darkening her powers, I felt growing concern and confusion about my new life in the Women's Healing Circle.

Chapter 2

Nearly two weeks later, on a chilly, overcast day in November, Isis and I set off in her aging red Dodge. I rode along as navigator and co-conspirator, clutching Flo's address and a map. Isis steered with a determined set to her jaw and paid no mind to the other drivers, which I found commendable. I had a tendency to fling insults at deserving offenders on the road, using an angelic expression on my face as cover.

"Are we getting close?" Isis asked, facing straight ahead, not even blinking in her concentration.

"It won't be long now. We're making good time. Too bad about the dark." Outside the dusk rapidly changed to darkness. No lighting from nature tonight, for this was the new moon. Waning moons were about letting go—of Flo?

"Couldn't be helped with our schedules. And we wouldn't have found Flo at home during the day with her agency job. We'll surprise her this way."

"So you think we'll find her?" A small wind chime tinkled from the rear view mirror. I wondered if I was supplying the wind.

"I hope so, Moonbeam. I really do." Her concern for Flo was touching, her tone serious. I wiggled in my seat, warm in my jeans, navy sweatshirt, and heavy red fleece jacket. Isis wore a purple sweat outfit with black jacket.

Most Circle members came from the east side of Pittsburgh, where Isis lived. I came from the west, and Flo was the only one who hailed from the north.

"Was the wicked witch from the north?" I asked.

"Where's the turnoff?" She gripped the steering wheel like it might get away.

"Sorry, I should have told you. It's a couple of miles yet, near a farm market, I think." The patchouli scent in her car soothed me. Isis believed in car aromatherapy.

"In answer to your question, which witch from the north?"

"You know—the *Wizard of Oz*."

"Oh. I don't think those were real witches. They were Hollywood witches."

"Never mind. Just thought there might be some correlation." I sat back and relaxed, but kept my eyes focused on the road.

"I hate to disappoint you, but the witches from the north and south were beautiful, wore prom gowns, and had the best special effects. East and west were the evil ones." Isis smiled and relaxed her death grip on the steering wheel.

"Rats. That shoots my theory. I was looking for some universal truth. Your version makes me one of the bad women."

"You can't trust Hollywood, Stephanie. Truth is often sacrificed for a better camera angle. Trust your own knowing, I always say."

I thought about movie and television witches and nodded my head in reply.

"Any more visions in the past week?"

I inhaled deeply and let it out slowly with a sigh. "No visions, thank you. I'd like to keep it that way. Slow down—there's the farm market." I had lived in the North Hills in past years, but Flo's particular address was a mystery. I hoped we could find it.

"Just go as slow as you can, and I'll check the mailboxes. I think we're getting near her number."

"Look on that mailbox—Pohaski," Isis said, deftly turning into a lane. "Is the number right?"

"Absolutely. Good job."

We drove through a wooded area, leaves strewn about the hillside. The lane headed up a slope to a house hidden from the road. The barren trees, stripped of their leaves, added to the starkness of the landscape. There were no neighboring houses. Isis pulled up in front of the house, leaving her car running and the headlights on, and we got out.

"I don't see her car, but there's a light on inside," she said.

The house resembled a summer cottage with its air of casual neglect, nestled in the woods. The white shutters hung slightly askew against the yellow siding. The wicker chairs and table on the front porch, a grimy white, needed cleaning.

I knocked politely on the front door.

"You're too ladylike," Isis said. She reared back and delivered deafening blows upon the door. I heard small creatures scurrying in the nearby underbrush.

We waited on the front porch.

I cannot say how long we waited, but we discussed upcoming meetings, and the air grew colder as we stood there. Periodically, Isis pounded on the door until finally she said, "I don't think she's here."

"Me, either. Let's go." I turned toward the car.

"I'll just try the door," she said, turning the doorknob vigorously.

"Isis! That's not a good idea."

"It's locked, anyway. How about peering in the windows? Is that a good idea?"

"Yes," I said, not sure why it was all right to peek but not to try door knobs. We went all around the house looking in, but saw nothing unusual, no signs or stirrings of life. Isis also tried the back door in our examination of Flo's house.

Our team of investigators reconvened by the car.

"There's only one thing we can do," she said in her usual matter-of-fact way.

"You mean call the police?"

"Something even more revealing than that. It's the New Age detective's greatest method of investigation."

"Consult the tarot cards?"

"Yes, we'll go straight to the cards. We could call where she works, though I'm not sure where that is, call the police, or whatever. But we'll get more information that's more accurate from the cards." Dead leaves blew across the driveway, sounding like applause for this advice.

"How about tonight? I don't have anything on the rest of today. That would work for me." I looked up, forgetting the new moon could not shed light onto our situation. Darkness reigned—the void, black and silent.

"Great. The sooner, the better. How about my house? Want to do a reading there?"

"Yes," I said, feeling strangely exhilarated. "We could do two readings. We could each do one."

"Never thought of that. I'm not sure Flo deserves all this attention, but yes, two spreads are better than one. Let's do it."

We rode in companionable silence back to Isis's home, wondering about the Flo we knew and could no longer find.

* * *

Nearly hidden in summer by the ancient maple in front, the big century-old house waited for us in darkness. The tree's branches brushed against me as I passed by, comforting as the touch of an old friend. Isis and I stood on the wide, comfortable porch as she unlocked the front door, then stepped inside and to the left to the ritual room.

We sat on the floor cross-legged, a deck of cards before each of us. The room felt mystical tonight, this study with its cabinets of books and heavy, dark, ornate furniture. Isis had lit dozens of cream candles perched in various parts of the room. Statues and figurines watched us from the mantel about the fireplace, and behind us the navy bead curtains jangled and moved, announcing the arrival of one of Isis's cats.

She rubbed up against me, purring, a short-hair red tabby.

"That's Shadow," Isis said, looking up from her shuffling of the cards. "The one I rescued from a garbage dumpster."

"No more foraging for food for you," I crooned to the curious cat. "You have a proper home now."

The other three cats were formidable in size, virtual couch pillow felines. I wondered if Shadow was destined for such an increase. Lean and healthy-looking, she'd just passed kittenhood.

"Interesting," Isis said as she laid out the cards in a standard Celtic cross formation.

I stopped petting Shadow, shuffled some more, and asked my question silently to the deck: What should we know about Flo and her disappearance? Then I cut the deck and laid out the cards quickly.

"This isn't what I expected," she muttered. "How about you?"

"I'm not sure about this. Maybe I should write mine down so I won't be influenced by your reading."

"Good idea." Isis got me a tablet and pen and I scribbled for a few minutes.

"I think I've got it," I said. "Do you mind going first?"

"Not at all." Isis read for her customers at the Mandala Book Store and was fluent with the tarot deck. I was somewhat less confident of my skills. I read for myself mainly during personal crises, which was often enough.

"I'm not sure what I expected," she continued, "but I'm accustomed to readings that are fairly tame. All along I've suspected a problem for Flo, but this looks worse than that. My overall feeling looking at this layout is confusion. Something or someone has shattered the foundations of Flo's world. See all the reversed cards," she pointed to the cards. "I feel fear and anxiety looking at this."

"You wouldn't tell Flo that if she were here getting a reading from you, would you?"

"No, of course not. But if she were here, the reading would look different. I see an ending here for her, and a new beginning. But I feel anxious about this new beginning; it feels false. I sense stagnant energies.

"These reversals give me an eerie feeling of blocked energies. It's as if she's being swallowed up back in time. If you look at this card, though, it seems to be part of a larger scheme, a divine pattern. Maybe she's finishing her end of a karmic debt."

"Perhaps." I was mesmerized, as I always was by Isis's readings.

"I'd really like to put these away," she said, quickly gathering up the cards. "I'll smudge the deck to clear it of these energies. Something feels deadly wrong. I can't quite place it. I'm just on the edge of something, but it's not coming through to me.

"I want to clear these cards," she mumbled again. "They're no good to me this way."

"Everything all right?" I asked.

"I'm pretty much okay, I think. Listen, maybe I'm wrong about all this. How about your reading?"

I looked at the sheet where I'd scribbled my impression of the cards.

"My thoughts are similar, though not shaded as darkly as yours. I see a karmic element—something Flo has done in this or a previous lifetime is cycling back to her. I see justice being dealt to her. She has made a choice that's not too good and the repercussions are washing over her like waves in a storm. It doesn't look like a happy ending, but perhaps a just one. For we know karma is the great equalizer. Karma evens the score, even if after a lifetime or more."

"Don't your cards feel dirty?" Isis asked, her forehead scrunched in concentration.

"No, but it feels dark and heavy, this information."

"Gather your deck up and I'll purify us both." She fanned out each deck on the center of the floor and lit a smudge stick, liberally perfuming all cards with burning sage. This was a thorough, almost compulsive smudging, not some token ritual. The pungent odor filled my senses.

When Isis had finished, she stood up and smiled. Her manner was lighter, as if a heavy burden had been lifted.

"Now shall we have some tea to mellow out our evening, Moonbeam?"

"Read my tea leaves?"

She laughed, and her hair looked especially blonde, and the light glinted off her gold nose ring.

"No tea leaves, friend. I'm using tea bags, and after this last reading, I might take a break from the business—learn to knit or something."

Chapter 3

The day before Thanksgiving broke bright and unseasonably warm. Tricksie and I enjoyed every moment we could on the front porch. I stretched out on the swing, savoring the sun warming my body, toeing the porch boards to keep it swaying. The portable phone lay clutched in one hand as I waited for an important phone call.

Tricksie, oblivious to phones and all human inventions (except cat food), teetered on the railing beside me. As usual, her feline charms bewitched my heart as she balanced and padded along lightly as a trapeze artist. Friendly breezes blew her long, soft black fur with beige tabby markings. She turned her wide face with the rusty owl eyes and contemplated the moving swing with a twitch of her tail.

Since my house had become Flo Search Headquarters, I'd experienced a surge of tension in my life. For a woman who had avoided conflict at all costs, this represented a major life change.

Keep it simple—my motto. I worked at Ruthie's Diner as a waitress at age thirty-eight. The degree in journalism lay buried somewhere in my unpretentious little house. This humble space was small and sturdy, just like me, only I didn't have two bedrooms, a garage, and white front and back porches. I had long, blonde hair—fly-away stuff, brown eyes, and pierced ears. I'd been told I'm cute, not attractive or beautiful. Makeup and fashion didn't suit me, except for my passion for gemstone jewelry. A diner waitress on my budget should stay away from jewelry stores and shows.

I steadied the swing with one foot, and Tricksie landed on my lap in one fluid motion. Moments later, the phone finally rang, we both jumped, and my cat disappeared around the corner of the house.

"Moonbeam, I just got your message. Is Flo really missing?"

"We think so, and we're tracking her down." I sighed in relief at Gretchen's voice. Gretchen had been coming to Circle meetings for many years, though she still looked like a college student in her long skirts and tank tops complemented by her long, straight, light brown hair. She spoke with conviction at our meetings, so I'd felt moved to contact her first regarding our Flo concerns.

"I noticed she'd stopped coming, but I just thought she'd found something else to do," Gretchen said.

"Isis has a strong feeling about this, plus we checked the cards, which showed major disaster. We tried to visit Flo at her house two weeks ago—no signs of life, not even a car. She's vanished, and we're searching for clues.

"Did you ever talk with her, learn anything about her family, close friends, maybe where she works?"

"I talked with her a time or two, though I didn't enjoy it because she was so negative. I tried to be a good little sister." I could picture

Gretchen's straight face, how the corners of her mouth could suddenly turn up as mischief sparked in her eyes.

"Remember when she'd unzip her jeans in the middle of a ritual and let her huge belly hang out. It was gross," I said. "Sorry, didn't mean to get negative myself."

Gretchen laughed, the chiming of tiny silver bells in her voice. "You and the rest of us were grossed out. Flo's family? She said they lived in Chicago, but that's all I know, so that's not really any help."

"Chicago? She told me Seattle."

"She mentioned Lake Michigan. I'm sure she said Chicago. She does social work in Oakland. Can't remember the name of the agency, but I can find out. My girlfriend's mother works there."

"I've hit the lottery. Does your girlfriend's mother know Flo?"

"Maybe recognize each other, that's about it. They work on different floors. Want the phone number?"

I felt instant relief, hoping our search was nearly ended. "We'd appreciate that, Gretchen. Isis can't stop worrying, and I'm beginning to get upset, too."

"I'll check with my girlfriend tonight and call you back. You and Isis always have my support and help." Her inner strength flowed through her words and I felt comforted.

I thanked her and hung up. Tricksie had again joined me on the swing, and I stroked her baby soft hair absent-mindedly.

Though I had difficulty caring for Flo due to her personality, I still felt at peace. I had never wished her any ill will, I just didn't enjoy talking with her or being around her. Her self-absorbed monologues during our meetings elicited a circle of yawns as her negativity infiltrated our proceedings designed to heal and promote self-empowerment.

My trusty cat helper delicately washed her face and front paws, gave me her knowing look, then leaped to the floor boards. She stood by the screen door, tail erect, waiting.

I glanced at my watch. "Right again, my friend. Just enough time to put on my waitress gear. I'm CEO of Ruthie's Diner, and I'll be expected."

"Mah," said Tricksie as I opened the door and she led me inside.

* * *

The dinner crowd cleared out before I had time to think of my answering machine. We hustled here at Ruthie's on Steubenville Pike, and I made an adequate living in the cozy atmosphere. It reminded me of my grandmother's house with its cheery flowered curtains and 50's décor—red vinyl covered kitchen chairs pulled up to black and chrome tables.

Honest, hard-working middle class people came to eat here, and they blended into the atmosphere. They sought the home cooking, for Ruthie's hands prepared mouth-watering meals. No one could dispute her mastery of cakes and pies.

"More coffee, Stephanie?" A man with white hair and beard sat at the counter, saluting me with his mug. "Glad Ruthie's is open tonight—Thanksgiving and all."

"Sure, Wilbur. How are you today?" I poured from a fresh pot, enjoying the enticing coffee aroma.

"Still wondering if this will be my last winter. Can't last forever, y'know."

"It isn't even winter yet. And look at that healthy head of hair. I bet you'll last at least a dozen more winters. What do you say, Orville?"

The white-haired man on the stool next to his brother looked up from a meatloaf sandwich and nodded.

"Yup," he said.

I quietly snorted at the two bachelor brothers who probably lived as reclusively as their namesakes Wilbur and Orville Wright had. These two had never learned to fly. They had been coming to the diner as long as I could remember, and I'd been working here the past six years.

The customers became my friends and the closest I had to family. They looked after me and I waited on them, occasionally listening to the concerns of their hearts. I was their mother, their sister, their aunt, their daughter—whatever the situation demanded.

"Say, what kind of pie do you have left?" I heard from the other end of the counter. He must have just sneaked in to the diner. I smiled at him. I wasn't waiting counter tonight, but these were my friends, and I couldn't deny them my services.

"Let's see, Hank. I've got chocolate mashed potato and beet cream pie that was dropped on the floor." My heart always skipped a few beats when I was near the lean man with mustache and salt-and-pepper bushy hair. He smelled like the forest—natural and woodsy.

"Then I'll take coconut cream, Stephanie. And cut a piece for yourself while you're at it." He patted the empty stool beside him.

"They all say I'm a cheap date. Ruthie even pays for my pie." I slid two gorgeous sugary concoctions onto the counter, moved around to the patron side, and hopped onto the stool. I put a welcoming hand on Hank's arm.

Bev nodded her head at me, signifying she'd cover my tables while I took my break. The first heavenly bite of pie sent my senses skyrocketing—delicate and sweet, like some exotic fruit. I'd have said better than sex, but I wasn't sure what that was any more.

I always enjoyed this old, familiar routine. Hank had come around for three years now, and we had been breaking together for two. We sat and chatted like an established couple, except our relationship was confined to the diner and this counter. Sometimes we sat at a table for variety.

We chatted companionably a few minutes before Hank cleared his throat and looked serious. He stared into my eyes. "I'd like to take you anywhere you want to go. To dinner at a fancy place if you like. Name the place and time." His green eyes shone steadily in the diner lights, intense, yet constant, and I knew he meant it.

Suddenly, invisible hands squeezed my throat, and my heart raced out of my chest. My face burned, like I'd just marched in from the desert.

"Did I say something wrong?" Hank asked, his pie forgotten.

I tried to talk to this man who was normally so easy to converse with. I tried to breathe, but the air wouldn't move. I hadn't expected it, this promise of a life beyond the diner.

Fear and anxiety, my companions in love, greeted me once again.

I nodded my head to my dear friend and his pie and scooted into the employee bathroom. I spied my remains—fiery red cheeks with underlying pallor, a sick, pinched look that was most unbecoming.

Breathing came in gasps at last, and when I'd recovered sufficiently, I tried to walk back into the dining room. Somehow I made a wrong turn and ended up in the lot behind the diner.

The crisp air felt good—rejuvenating--and I breathed deeply of it, taking care to slow the breaths. I could see my rust-enhanced blue Escort, and I fought a strong impulse to rush to it and peel out. Besides, my jacket, purse, and the car keys were stashed in the diner.

After ten minutes of mindful breathing, I came back from whatever state I'd been in.

Not again. I got worse as I grew older, and I wasn't that old.

I just couldn't seem to do it. No matter how hard I tried, I couldn't successfully navigate the waters of a relationship. I couldn't even get started.

Maybe I shouldn't be alarmed about my condition, my disorder—whatever it is. I lived a good life, and Tricksie and I celebrated every day together. I was happy settling for that and my customers at the diner.

Then, coming back to planet earth, I thought, what must Hank think of me?

He appeared from around the building in response to my telepathic question, his expression guarded. My anxiety level hiked up several notches as I smiled weakly at him and waited for harsh words and angry gestures. He stopped several yards from me, his hands clenched at his sides.

My hands, knees, and insides were all quivering.

Chapter 4

"Stephanie, I didn't know," he said, his green eyes glowing.

"Know what?" My body shook in anticipation of the scene.

"I should have known when you were content to be my diner buddy. Maybe I sensed something even then. I let us drift along without trying to get closer. You realize most women would have expected a date, a real one, years ago."

"I guess I'm not most women. Hank, I'm sorry I ran out like that. I have to go back to work." The anxiety cranked up another notch.

"It's a phobic reaction, Steph," he said. He took both my hands into his, and my shivering subsided. "It'll be all right. Go back to work, then."

Gratitude flowed into me like a mountain-fresh stream. Hank understood. No one before had. Hank and I were still friends.

My hands still warm from his, I waved and stepped through the back door of the diner. I saw the phone and remembered my messages. I had wanted to phone home on my break to see if Gretchen had left the information about Flo. No time now, for my break had extended too long already.

You're probably just out there flying around on your broom, Sister Flo. I'll check on you later.

Somehow, the thought of Flo struggling to sit upright on her broom gave me hope and I felt a smile relaxing my face. Of course, real witches don't fly on brooms.

* * *

I played the message once more and copied down the phone number.

"Here's the information, Moonbeam. My friend just got back to me. Flo works at the Helping Hands Agency. Her department helps with job placement for the disabled and mentally challenged. My friend's mother didn't know the phone number for Flo, but the number for the agency should get you there. It's 555-3133.

"Good luck with your investigation. Blessed be."

"Thank you, Miss Gretchen. You're a life saver," I said to the machine.

Tricksie leaped onto the bed where I'd stretched out and batted at the strings of my hooded jacket. I hugged her briefly because she doesn't like too much squeezing. She's truly a gift because she mysteriously appeared one day outside my little green house.

At first I just set food out for her, hoping she'd survive, but go away. Usually I sent the men in my life away and kept my lifestyle simple, but this was an enchanting long-haired creature. When it rained, I brought her in. She'd appeared out of nowhere, like a magic trick, so

I named her Tricksie. Later, she would perform amazing cat tricks that would justify that name.

She would vanish in the house for hours on end, and I could never find her hiding place. She could slip outside without my knowledge, later reappearing on the back doorstep to my surprise. For a slightly plump eleven-pound cat, she was amazingly tricky, fast, and sneaky.

I had begun searching for my past roots, reading books on healing methods before Tricksie came. Why I didn't recognize her as a witch's cat right from the start is beyond me. She wasn't just any random stray.

Flashes of insight since then have convinced me she was my cat helper in a past lifetime, when I was a flaming, forest-seeking witch. We operated together in a dynamic way. I often wondered if in the next lifetime Tricksie will be the witch and I the cat helper.

That's why I'm especially good to her. I shower her with catnip toys to make up for not recognizing her in the first place.

As I raised myself up to reach for the phone, she attacked the hood strings viciously, narrowly missing my face.

"Watch it, Tricks. I've got to call Isis. She'll want to hear the news, even if it's late. This can't wait."

"Of course it's not too late," she said when I got her on the line. "I was doing a tarot reading for myself before bedding down. Actually, I was thinking about you and the Flo situation when the phone rang. What's up?"

"I called Gretchen and her friend's mother works in the same building as Flo. Gretchen got me the number of the agency—simpler than I expected." I felt proud of my detective work.

"What was it?"

"555-3133," I read off the paper.

"No, the name of the agency."

"The Helping Hands Agency. Job placement for those difficult to place."

"That would be me. Maybe I should hire Flo." Other than her card readings, Isis was unemployed and rarely held a job. She had gone from rearing children to a divorce and then to a long term relationship with her college professor.

I laughed, which eased any lingering tension over Hank and our scene together.

"Who would run the metaphysical events if you got a job? Besides, maybe Flo could find me a job more suited to my education. Big laugh."

"You have a degree in journalism, don't you, Moonbeam?"

"I graduated with distinction and I've worked in diners and restaurants most of my adult life. I can proofread a menu with the best of them." My light-hearted attitude was genuine, for I'd always loved and never regretted my work. "Waitress life seems to suit me. I'm still wondering what I'm going to be when I grow up."

"Maybe you could write mysteries set in a diner."

"Maybe I'd better let you finish your reading. We have enough mystery in our lives right now. Just wanted to tell you about Flo. I'll call Helping Hands in a few days. Have a good Thanksgiving."

Isis cleared her throat purposefully, and I knew she had something important to say. Her conversations were jammed with purpose and meaning.

"There's something I haven't told you, Stephanie. Flo and I fell out. Could figure into her disappearance." Her uneasiness wafted through the phone receiver.

"What happened?"

"One night at Circle, it was just Flo and me. Kate came later—much later. Circle attendance nose-dived for several months, and I thought Flo's negativity might have scared them off. So I decided to talk it over with her, especially since it was just the two of us."

"You have more nerve than I do. That sounds like dangerous territory." I smiled at the thought of a showdown between the two of them.

"I think I was being tactful, not rude or insensitive. I tried to get her to face up to her behavior in the group, so that she could see it from our perspective. I honestly can't remember the exact words used." Her voice trailed off as if she remembered unpleasantness.

"Did Flo react to your speech?"

"Oh, yes. She clearly got the point. She got madder and madder as I spoke. She jumped up at one point, her pants flying open. Her big belly hung out. She wanted to yell at me, I know, but for the longest time she just turned red, fumed, and shook a finger at me.

"Finally, I said, 'Flo, I'm not trying to make you mad or exclude you from the group. You need to be aware how your behavior affects everybody. If you become aware of the negativity, you can deal with it. We are here to find positive pathways for our lives, to learn self-empowerment. That doesn't leave any room for singing the blues week after week.'

"'I am not negative,' Flo said, her belt ends flopping. 'You're the negative one. All high and mighty, telling us all what to do like some Egyptian queen. Who are you to tell me how to act or what to say?'

"At that point—miracle of miracles—the door opened, and Kate came in, just when things got out of control. She turned to me and then Flo and said, 'My, where is everybody? What's the program tonight?'"

"Kate must have sensed something was going on," I said.

"She did. Her presence was enough to deflate Flo. She just zipped her pants, muttered to herself and gathered up her stuff. Kate tried to talk with her, but she cast evil looks on both of us. Flo said one last thing as she left." Isis sounded uncomfortable.

"I'm afraid to ask."

"She said, 'You and this whole circle of women be damned,' then she slammed the door."

"Hmmm. That does change the complexion of this story. I understand why Flo wouldn't want to be in contact with us. Maybe we should assume she's just avoiding us and that our search is over." I felt relieved, for I'd have more time for chasing Tricksie in the house.

"I'm worried about her, and she's probably doing incantations so our boobs will fall off." We laughed till I felt tears in my eyes.

"But seriously, Moonbeam, my intuition and the cards lead me in a different direction. I still think something else is going on here, even though Flo disappeared right after our confrontation. I don't know what's happening, but she's in danger. We may be in danger, too."

I swallowed hard as Isis shared her feelings, and I got an eerie feeling somewhere around my midsection.

"Isis," I asked, spooked by her talk of Flo and danger. "But what can we do? How can we approach this problem if we have no idea what's going on?

Chapter 5

Thanksgiving had been pretty low key, just Tricksie and me. I'd brought home turkey dinner from the diner and fed the meat to her, which she devoured with great enthusiasm. The pumpkin pie, not too sweet and nice and spicy, sustained me, as well as big portions of mashed potatoes, stuffing, and a dab of cranberry sauce. I could taste Ruthie's love in every bite.

We watched old movies on television and I wrote about my thanks, for I was grateful for my job at Ruthie's, my new friends at the Women's Healing Circle, my happy little home, and especially for little Miss Tricksie. As I finished writing about my gratitude for her, she rubbed her head against my hand that held the pen, her thanks in return for mine.

Black Friday dawned cold, but bright, and the sun's rays gave me hope that answers lay ahead. I could see a few stray snowflakes outside from our bed, and Tricksie lay in the curve of my arm, purring with abandon. Tricksie did everything with abandon. So far I hadn't learned nearly enough from my cat. Mostly all that had rubbed off were her dark, fuzzy hairs.

"What do you predict for today?" I asked her on this important day for shoppers and business owners as I patted her head and back. I liked to get the day report first thing so I could decide whether or not to get out of bed.

This report seemed good. Tricksie kept purring madly. That meant an excellent day, certainly a better one than yesterday.

Wednesday. I tried to forget about the scene with Hank and my talk with Isis. I vaguely remembered promising to call the agency where Flo worked to find her, even though it sounded like she and Isis were feuding.

Tricksie lured me out of bed so I could feed her. I puttered about the house and lost a few hours before I got serious about my mission. "I'm going to call the agency," I told my cat helper who seemed more interested in her cardboard cat scratcher from Wal-Mart. I savored the heady aroma and taste of the last bite of a bagel-to-die-for.

"I'll just talk with the operator instead of Flo," I added and picked up the phone. She didn't look up from a vicious attack on a gray catnip mouse as she rolled on her back.

Since Flo had shunned our group, I hoped to avoid any hostility. On the other hand, I had never been unpleasant with Flo, I had merely avoided her, like the plague of misery she was.

I dialed and the phone rang.

"Hello, Helping Hands Agency. How may I help you?" The voice sounded compassionate and pleasing, very un-Flo-like.

"Hi. I wanted to ask about Flo Pohaski."

"One moment, please."

I panicked, figuring the operator had connected me with Flo's extension. I fought a nearly overwhelming impulse to hang up.

"This is Janice Wilson. May I help you?" Her voice healed my anxiety, and I felt instant relief. Whoever she was, she was better than talking to Flo.

"Yes, I'm Stephanie Gray. I know Flo Pohaski from our women's group. We haven't heard from her for several weeks now, and we're concerned about her. Have you any information on her?"

"Yes, I've been telling everyone that Flo no longer works here."

"I see. How long has she been gone?"

"Several weeks—six or more, I'd say."

I felt stumped, but not beaten yet. "Where has she gone?"

"She left no forwarding address. I wouldn't be at liberty to give out any more information, anyway, even if I knew. Ms. Pohaski wasn't very friendly with the staff. If she had a close friend here, I'd give you the name. She kept to herself."

Totally bewildered, I thanked the helpful lady and hung up.

So our big lead wasn't a lead after all. There seemed no way of tracking Flo, and frankly, I was tiring of the ordeal.

Flo was just as difficult in her absence as she had been in our presence.

* * *

The lights seemed especially bright that evening at Ruthie's Diner, so that every French fry and ball of fuzz on the rug was highlighted, wrinkles on hard-working patrons accentuated, and dirt on chubby children's hands illuminated.

Or maybe my imagination soared, my awareness heightened by extra adrenalin pumped into my body. For Hank, who had been a steady source of comfort to me, now served as the object of my anxiety. I stood here, working my shift assisting the hungry and soul weary, feeling uneasy.

What if Hank came by like he usually did? What would I do? What would I say? How could I possibly face him?

"Rosemary, can you give me a cigarette?" I asked my co-worker, a pretty dark-haired Italian girl.

"Sure, Steph, but you don't smoke. You don't even eat meat. You're into all that healthy stuff." Her gold neck chains reflected wildly in the bright light.

"Thanks," I said as she handed me a filter-tipped cigarette.

"Let's go in the back. I'll light it for you."

In our crowded break room, Rosemary flicked a lighter and efficiently lit my cigarette, the smoke assaulting my senses. She was always efficient, friendly, caring, and uplifting. If I were to take on another friend, it would be Rosemary. But she was too busy for that, anyway, with her husband, two small children, and family get-togethers.

"Now this is your affair, friend, but I was here and I know about that Hank business. Can I help you with that?"

"Some of us are beyond help." I took a drag on the cigarette, and then coughed the sooty air from my lungs. I had never been a smoker, and this attempt at tension release was rapidly failing.

"You don't have to be afraid of Hank. He's totally harmless and one of the few really nice guys I've met in my life." Rosemary had been working at the diner longer than I had and was a good judge of character.

"I agree with you. Everything you say is true. But the problem isn't with Hank. The problem is with me."

"I don't get that, Stephanie. You're a wonderful, warm-hearted person. You're practically a saint, the way you treat the customers in this diner."

I smiled at Rosemary and her vote for my sainthood. "That's because in the whole world, other than my cat and the women's group I belong to, I don't have a life. This diner is my life."

"But look at how you and Hank spend time together. You look like a happily married couple—minus the children. I thought you liked him."

I knew what this was—not an interrogation or invasion of my privacy, but a caring friend helping me work through the issues. I was suddenly glad the diner business was slow tonight.

"Sure, I like him. I value his friendship. Of course, in some ways I don't know him very well. I've never seen him outside the diner. Well, maybe in the parking lot."

"What does he do? Where does he live? Is he much older than you? I used to talk with him a little, but after you came, he focused on you." Rosemary drew deeply on one of her cigarettes, and I wondered if she smoked because she was too perfect in every other way.

"He teaches at Community College—creative writing and English. He lives somewhere in the woods toward Weirton, but this diner is on his route home. As far as age, he might be fifty, maybe less, but older than me by at least ten years. I never asked.

"Nothing about him turns me off or would prevent a relationship. The fact is I can't get close to a man. I had a brief disastrous marriage when I was young, and ever since then I've been skittish. I've given up on the idea. It's nice that you care enough to talk this over with me." I was beginning to wonder if my customers needed me. I listened for my name being called.

Rosemary took another soulful drag off her cigarette. Her pretty face looked troubled, and she said, "But you're such a great person and so is he. I don't understand why it can't just happen. You know, like in the movies."

I laughed, stood up, and pointed around the crowded little room.

"Does this look like the movies, Rosemary?"

She pouted ever-so-slightly. "It could be, Steph. It could be just exactly like a movie. Maybe even better."

When I stopped coughing from my last inhaled smoke-breath, I smiled tenderly at her.

"I hope you're right, my friend. Clear to the bottom of my being, I hope you're absolutely right."

* * *

The rest of the night crept by as I tried to keep busy, to stop staring at the door each time it opened. Even though I feared facing Hank again, I feared his absence even worse.

After all, he was just a customer. I didn't even have a phone number where I could call him. I waited counter tonight, too, so I was painfully aware he wasn't on his stool. Sometimes we sat at a table, but mostly we sat at the counter.

"Maybe he couldn't make it tonight. Maybe he had to work late," Rosemary said as we restocked the stations with sugar, artificial sweetener, and packets of condiments.

"He always came when I was here. He rarely missed." I tried not to sound too depressed.

"He didn't come in when you weren't here. Did you know that?"

"Funny, I never even thought about that. He usually came in even when I worked extra, when we were short of help. But, no, Rosemary, I guess I thought he came in when I wasn't here."

"He'll be back. If not tonight, then soon."

"I must have really scared him or made him mad. I didn't expect he'd bail out on me." I tried hard not to sound disappointed.

"You scared yourself worse. And you came back," Rosemary said. She compressed her lips and considered her next words. "I think he loves you, dear. Sometimes I can see it in his eyes. Your little scene didn't change that."

The rest of the night I watched and waited, feeling abandoned, though our relationship was strictly informal and mostly imaginary.

That night I dreamed I was in an elegant restaurant. Sitting at the bar was Hank, dressed in suit and tie. Beside him sat a young, attractive waitress, and Hank slid an arm around her shoulders. I watched helplessly as they laughed and flirted together, and I realized that I never wanted Hank more than now when he was gone.

Chapter 6

I stood amidst the people sensing the terrific energies in this space, feeling a peace and contentment despite the activities. I closed my eyes momentarily, and I imagined myself on a grassy hill in the sun, surrounded by daffodils, the flowers and my hair lifted by playful breezes. The place felt sacred, though we hadn't yet invoked the God or Goddess or cast the circle. I knew our ritual would be special tonight.

We joined the Druids tonight at Friends' Meeting House for the celebration of Yule on the winter solstice, when the days begin to lengthen and the sun returns to us. I arrived promptly at 7:45 p.m. for a 7 p.m. ritual because Druids were never on time. Even now, the leaders still set up for the ritual.

Druids must surely live in the moment.

I gazed around the parlor with its fireplace and grand piano and was rewarded by the smiling faces of some of my Circle members: Maria, Gretchen, and Christi Lee. I felt a warmth at seeing them that rivaled the candlepower around us. The slightly shabby appearance of this room was masked by the romantic light of our candles. For they alone lit the space—huge green pillar candles on the mantel, cream candles in tall metal stands, and a silver candelabra with red tapers on the piano.

All around lay holly greens, festive and timely, promising the eternal greenness that perpetuates life. A whiff of pine scent from somewhere reached my nose, and I gratefully inhaled.

I gazed around again for the tenth time, looking for Isis, who usually greeted me when I arrived at an event. The Druid leaders caught my eye as they labored over the red altar cloth on the floor. A big woman in white robe with long, gray hair placed items beside the silver candlesticks with red taper candles. I idly hoped her hair and the flickering flames wouldn't make contact.

I nearly rushed over, and then her husband in matching white robe grabbed the long, gray tresses and spoke to her. He looked mischievous with his pot belly, brown mustache, and pointed beard.

I became so involved in the hair drama, that when I felt the hand on my shoulder, I jumped.

"Did you miss me?" Isis said quietly as she sat down on the floor beside me. She looked especially lively tonight in a red sequined top with long, tight red skirt. The thigh-high slit up one side enabled her to assume her usual floor position with only minimal squiggling.

She patted the hair pulled up on her head, and readjusted the holly wreath topping it all. Altogether, she looked a bit flashier than our altar.

"I wondered if you were coming," I said. "I've never beaten you to the ritual before. By the way, you look great."

"Trying to go mainstream takes more time and effort than I remembered. I probably won't attempt this look again for another five years. You look pretty, yourself," she said, nodding toward my green velvet jumper and cream blouse.

My outfit felt stodgy compared to hers, but still appropriate to this ritual.

"Thanks, friend," I said, readjusting my crossed legs for comfort's sake. She smiled and started to ask me something, but the Druids, at long last, were beginning. They moved to the beat of some internal Druid time awareness.

I looked around the elongated circle with the altar in the center and estimated that about forty of us were seated on the floor. John, the leader in the white robe with the mischievous smile, motioned for us to rise. I'd run extra miles at the diner this week, so I hoisted it up with considerable effort and a grunt. I wondered if I'd have to leave our Circle when my knees gave out, which could be any moment now.

Four of us sang notes to open the four gateways, or directions, to cast our circle. I sang the west gateway, my note mellow and sustained, crystal clear and loud in the quieted room. I felt at home as John invoked the God and Goddess to bless our ritual.

The Druids proved wordier and more ceremonious in their ritual than we witches. Still, we sang songs and participated with joy. Karen, the leader's wife with the long gray hair, clothed in matching white robe, lit a large cream candle shaped like the sun in the center of the altar. Her melodious voice rose and filled the room with hope as she spoke.

"Say goodbye to the longest night and the shortest day of our year. Now the sunlight returns to us. Each day the sun floods our lives with precious energy.

"We celebrate rebirth this Yule; though winter is still before us, throughout the snowy days, the light returns to us. Each year each of us celebrates new beginnings. Our lives are reborn in so many ways. Please, let us take a few minutes to meditate on new beginnings or rebirth in our lives."

The light glowed softly around her white and gray form as if she shone with some inner light. I closed my eyes reluctantly, for this scene was beautiful and soul-enriching. I imagined Karen to be some kind of urban angel hovering over our houses and apartments, keeping us safe. Then, I looked inward in the silence of this group, basking in the energy of us all. I tried to keep my mind uncluttered, yet focused on our subject.

New beginnings—that would be Tricksie, Isis, and the Women's Healing Circle. It all sprouted in the past year.

And then I felt a longing, like an ache, in my heart. I hadn't seen or heard from Hank in over three weeks, since that evening at the diner.

Lost people. This meditation should be about those missing in action. Maybe we could all meditate them back into our lives. First Flo, now Hank. I hoped no one else would disappear.

My eyes closed, I sensed those near me, heard someone clear his throat, and smelled the burning candles. Then I heard a distinct rustling of dried leaves as if underfoot, felt cool breezes around me, smelled rich earth, and heard a lark sing. I opened my eyes and looked up into the face of a tall man in black hooded robe. We stood in a clearing by a thickly wooded area, and I automatically rose to greet him.

The hood fell back, and his face jolted me, for he gazed into my eyes with tremendous love and tenderness. I caught my breath and nearly missed seeing his sturdy frame and hands, the curly brown hair, the unremarkable features.

Unremarkable except for his eyes, burning love into me like never before, branding my heart. He reached for me, and I closed my eyes again, feeling confused by his emotion. Something about him, though, compelled me to receive his love. In my heart, I felt magnetically drawn to this man who was so much a stranger, yet familiar at the same time.

The Druids droned on, reciting yet another lengthy piece. I opened my eyes again, back at Friends' Meeting House. All stood in our oblong circle, all except me, and I quickly rose. The disorientation I always felt after a vision lasted for ten or fifteen minutes, a mere blink of an eye for a Druid.

I glanced sideways at Isis, who raised her eyebrows and mouthed, "What happened?" I smiled and turned to watch John and Karen at the altar.

Then, by some modern-day miracle, the ritual finished. We filed into a side room where refreshments set out on a long table tantalized us.

My legs felt wobbly beneath the green velvet skirt as I tried to socialize. At the back of my mind, the vision lingered, destroying my focus. I considered holing up in the bathroom when Isis approached me.

She stared pointedly, and said, “Something happened again, didn’t it? You were a million miles away.”

I felt relief at her concern, though I still wrestled with the images. “I don’t know where I was, maybe hundreds of years back in time, across the ocean, I think. I was with someone—that was the main idea this time. He loved me with a burning passion. I don’t understand that kind of love.”

“There’s a message in it for you, and you’ll just have to piece all the messages together to make sense of it. What a happy thought, this loving man,” she said as she put a grounding hand on my arm.

I nodded, but I wondered if it was really a happy thought. Great love made me a little uncomfortable. It came to others, but not to me.

“You look oh so sophisticated tonight, Isis, like a cover girl, except for the nose ring,” I said, glad to shift the conversation from myself.

“Thank you, dear. With all this holiday bustle, we’ve lost touch with each other. I haven’t thought much about Flo. I think I’m behind on the latest happenings.”

"I'm sorry I haven't made it to Circle these past few weeks. A few things came up." I didn't want to tell her I'd slid into a deep depression over Hank and was hiding in my house.

"Not too many at Circle. Everybody's busy getting ready for the holidays. My family's coming over on Christmas day, so I've cleaned and cleaned. I'm fixing turkey dinner for eighteen."

My jaw dropped. "That doesn't sound like you. Does a High Priestess of healing who doesn't eat meat stuff a turkey?"

She laughed, and the sequins looked like flashing faceted precious gems.

"Evidently so. I'm resurrecting my pre-vegetarian self for this. I love my family, though I'm not too big on all the work. I'm basically trying to be normal for one day." She made a funny little scrunched-up face.

"Good luck. You can do it," I said. Normal wasn't her strong point and probably not mine, either.

"So tell me, Moonbeam, what's the latest on Flo? You had her work number, as I remember. Did you call her there?"

"Yes, I called and I thought they were going to connect me to her, but I needn't have worried about that."

"She wouldn't talk to you?" Druids moved around us, selecting holiday treats, but we concentrated intensely so that we barely noticed them.

"I can't say. Flo doesn't work there anymore. She quit."

Isis looked stumped, not a natural state of being for her.

"This is so very odd. I can see why she might not communicate with us here at Circle, especially me. But why would she quit her job? This isn't making any sense. After Christmas we'll get to the bottom of this."

"But how?" I asked her gently. Our investigation faced a corner, with no place to go.

"We'll worry about how later," Isis said. "We'll just figure this out somehow. And there's one more thing."

"What?"

"There's something going on with you. There's such an air of sadness about you. I can sense some trauma. It's as if you've lost your best friend."

"Very close. I think you win a cigar." My smile felt tired and forced.

"I hope it's one of those slim ones with the plastic tip. What's going on?"

I told her briefly about Hank, our confrontation, and his absence from the diner for weeks. As I talked I felt a few tears sliding down my face, and my throat choked up until I could barely get the words out.

"Poor Stephanie," she said.

"I didn't know I cared this much. For some reason I'm getting all emotional about this. He's just a customer." I sniffled, tears dotting my munchie plate. I used a napkin with holly patterns on it to wipe away all traces of my love sickness.

Love. Did I really love Hank? Is that what this was all about?

"Moonbeam, he isn't just a customer, not from what you've said. This is serious. It's about deep, honest feelings of love for this man. If you're in love with him, it'd be natural to ache for him now."

"I try not to think about it too much. He was always just a customer." Was I lying to myself?

"You may want to meditate on that, about Hank and who he is to you, what he means to you. Some of us keep the emotional gates closed tight against others, keep our guard up and others at a distance. That doesn't mean we don't have feelings for others. It means the feelings are so buried, we may not even know what we feel." Isis spoke gently, with great respect for my person, as if she personally knew where I was coming from.

"I guess you're right, Isis. I didn't realize he meant anything to me. I'll try to sort it out, but it may not make any difference, anyway." I sighed and put down the plate of delicacies.

"You mean because he's gone?"

"Yes. As in no trace of Hank. I don't know if he's ever coming back."

"But your feelings need to be faced and felt. They need to be released, one way or the other. I don't think you have much to worry about. He's coming back. He won't be able to stay away, even if he wanted to."

"You have a feeling about this?"

"Very strong. He's coming back. It won't be as you expect, but it will be better than anything you've known before. In fact, it will be a whole new creation—something so beautiful I can't describe it."

Isis shook herself, and I felt shimmery shocks of energy roller coasting up and down my spine.

"I'm feeling jealous of your love life, Steph. Burt and I have a more good friend-like arrangement." Burt was her partner, a man eighteen years her senior. They lived together in his big century-old house that I had grown to love.

"Nothing to be jealous of right now. On the contrary, I feel pretty pathetic."

She hugged me soundly, Druids or no Druids.

"Wait and see," she said.

"What about Flo?" I asked, hoping to divert attention from myself. Enough of being in the spotlight.

"We'll take care of that after the holidays. It's time to bring the Circle in on this. We need reinforcements."

I poured us each a paper cup of punch.

"Here's to reinforcements," I said as we saluted paper cups, a dull toast with a papery clink.

"And here's to Moonbeam and a special customer, and to love and happily-ever-after," Isis said, repeating our silent toast.

My smile was still unconvincing, especially to me, but I felt better already. Her words brought me much-needed comfort.

Yule—the Druids said it symbolized rebirth. Perhaps this Yule would symbolize the rebirth of my long-forgotten hopes and dreams for love.

Chapter 7

I stepped back from my labors and looked at the results. I thought it looked spectacular.

"What do you think, Tricksie? Do you like it?" She must have, because she lay on her back and batted a stocking ornament. I knew if I didn't place it higher on the tree she'd eventually have it off and chewed up.

Earlier, when I'd started to put together this manufactured tree, with just two of the lower branches in place, Tricksie had hunkered beneath them like some forest creature.

I knew the artificial tree would be all right then.

I'd wavered because I'd always had a real tree before, but I hated struggling with it and coercing it into a tree stand. Yes, this fake evergreen would do the job, though I missed the heady smell of pine.

From my CD player strains of "Silent Night" swelled, and I gathered Tricksie into my lap on the floor and sang to her. After one verse, she left, but listened from beyond my reach under the tree.

This was the only time of year I couldn't relinquish all my Christian ways. I remembered my childhood when we'd sung

Christmas carols and gone to Christmas Eve church service, a candlelight service that I found especially magical.

But we women and the Druids held candlelight services all the time and sang songs. And the Christmas tree was basically a pagan tradition.

"Maybe I'm not missing so much after all, Tricksie." She batted a purple ball ornament. "Well, pagan or not, merry Christmas Eve, my sweetie."

Ruthie's Diner had closed at six that evening for the holiday and wouldn't reopen until the morning after Christmas. At first, I had hoped to work—I like spending holidays with customers. But now that I was home with the cat, it all seemed so festive and right.

Tricksie and I got excited about every little thing. It didn't take much to amuse us.

Of course, Isis had invited me to her house, a customer to hers, and even my neighbor Tony had made an offer, but I still felt that sadness that weighed at my heart. I didn't want to be a part of a room of people, especially mostly people I didn't even know. I would stay home this year.

"I thank the universe for you, my furry friend. If it weren't for you, I'd be all alone." I shivered as Tricksie rolled around on the floor with the stocking ornament. Maybe without this lovable cat I would have opted for the room full of people I didn't know.

“Silent night, holy night,” spilled from the stereo speakers as I wrestled with Tricksie for the sock. In our scuffling, I almost missed the doorbell.

I answered it, not knowing who to expect, maybe a customer.

He stood on the front porch looking uncomfortable, wearing brown corduroys, a brown leather jacket with fur collar, and no hat. Snowflakes pelted him, the big, fluffy variety that were a festive holiday item at this moment.

“I think it might be a white Christmas,” he said as a big flake hit him in the eye. He shifted a bag with a bottle to the other hand.

“Hank, this is a nice surprise. Please come in. You’re just in time for the celebration.”

He entered and I took his jacket, hanging it on a dining room chair. I was on edge already, yet relieved to see him. Questions filled my head, but outwardly I was collected, saying, “Please sit down. Can I get you something to drink? Want some fruitcake?”

“We’re not at the diner. You don’t have to wait on me.” He sat stiffly on the couch and put the bag on the floor. I was pointedly aware he’d never been in my house before.

“No, really. Something to drink?”

“Not now, Steph. It took all my courage and then some to stop here. I’d better explain a few things.” His expression was at best guarded. This was hardly the pleasant companion of the last few years at the diner. Some stranger had taken his place.

“How did you find me? I never told you where I live.”

Tricksie had landed on the dining room table and cautiously approached Hank's jacket. She gingerly smelled the fur on the collar. I held my breath, hoping she wouldn't attack the poor deceased creature.

"I called the diner this morning and Rosemary answered. I asked how to find you, and after a slight pause, she gave me great directions. She wished me luck."

"I've missed you, Hank. I thought you were mad at me." My face felt hot, and I hoped I wouldn't cry.

"No, I wasn't mad. You didn't do anything wrong."

"Just a minute," I said as I gently removed Hank's jacket from Tricksie's admiring eyes and filed it in the closet.

"Now, what became of you?" I asked as I rearranged myself on my green chair. Hank sat beside me on the beige sofa. My living room was comfortable, a little cluttered, and clean, but not elegant. Nothing about my house was sophisticated, but I liked it that way.

"I got called out to work," he said, shifting his gaze to his hands. "I have this other job I sometimes do."

"I know. Sometimes you're gone over a weekend or a day here or there, but I've never known you to go for…it's been a month. Must have been a big job."

I wanted to ask about this other job, but he'd never offered any information before, and I hated to pry.

Hank must have read my mind.

"Since I've been gone so long, I thought I needed to offer you an explanation, Stephanie. I wanted to call you and explain sooner, but I was kept busy with the job. We're constantly on the move."

I smiled and patted Tricksie, who had shifted to the living room since the fur had crawled away. She was eying Hank, but hadn't made her move yet.

"But confidentiality is important in this work. I still hesitate to speak of it. Let me just say that I've done the work for years. It's a nice opposite to my work in academia. To study and learn is one thing, but for this, I'm moving, breathing, more alive."

His face and gestures were so animated that I smiled in response.

"That's how I feel when I participate in our rituals. I've gone to Protestant churches all my life, and I've fallen asleep, fidgeted, and studied the people in the congregation.

"Now I feel a part of the earth with the Healing Circle. Our rituals are magical, and I'm intensely interested in them. A strong energy pulls me into this, an energy that correlates with ancient oak trees, hawks soaring high, and palm trees filtering the breezes."

I stopped. "Why am I telling you all this?"

Now he smiled. "I'm glad you shared your feelings. I've attended pagan events. I admired the ideas and intent of the rituals, but I never felt that strong pull."

"You said you were working. What about your job at the college?" I asked.

"I had some time off coming, and our Christmas break began early. I can usually get time off."

Tricksie had sniffed Hank during our conversation, and must have considered him one of us, for she slowly crept onto his lap. I hoped her dark fur would be unnoticeable on the dark brown corduroy. He didn't seem to notice her arrival.

"I didn't come here to talk about my second job." Hank stared straight into my eyes, and I marveled at his deep emerald gaze.

"I haven't had time to think about why you're here. I'm still in shock." I could feel my shoulders tightening up.

"I didn't call you. I don't have your phone number, but Rosemary would have given it to me. I didn't want to give you time to disappear or tell me to go away."

"But you did go away, and I didn't like it. I worried that you were never coming back." Was this any way to talk to a loyal customer?

"Maybe I just needed time to sort things out. Maybe I took the work just to get away. I've admired you for a long, long time." His voice dropped, and I felt my cheeks flush.

"So you didn't have to take the job after all."

"They're all optional. I've turned down many interesting jobs so I can sit in the diner with you or watch you work. I'm not sure how to handle this conversation or even what to say to you.

"But damn it, Stephanie, I'm not going to act like nothing has happened."

He petted Tricksie, and I began to get that tight feeling about my chest and throat, and all I could think of was, help me somebody. I need someone to play my part for me, to keep me from weirding out

Chapter 8

"I thought we could celebrate, this being Christmas Eve and all." Hank pulled a bottle of champagne from his bag. "Or did you have other plans, Stephanie? I don't want to intrude on your holiday or your plans."

The green bottle caught my attention. Champagne sounded like a pretty good idea at this point—something to take the edge off acute anxiety.

"You guarantee that's a good year?" I asked.

"Not only a good year, but also, it's French champagne. You'll find it superior to the California champagnes, at least it was in price."

I smiled in spite of any discomfort. This was the Hank I had grown to love at the diner—a good and interesting companion and someone who stirred my primal urges. I rummaged in the kitchen cabinets for my good lead crystal wine glasses with the gold ring around their rims.

I presented Hank with the corkscrew, which had been buried in the utensil drawer. I wasn't sure if I still had one. The few alcoholic beverages I consumed had screw tops, a certain sign of their elegance.

"It's all right for me to stay for a while, Steph?" he asked, his hand smoothing Tricksie's fur.

"Yes, and I'm glad you're here. I thought Tricksie and I were going to be alone. I had invitations, but staying here seemed right. I didn't feel like mingling with strangers."

"Let me open the champagne, then." Hank stumbled up from the couch, Tricksie flying.

If this had been the movies, I would have fallen in his arms right then and there. In fact, this little scene ran through my head, and Rosemary would have been proud of me. I saw us melting into each other's arms, murmuring words of love and appreciation, feeling pure animal lust for one another.

But instead, I saw Tricksie hit the rug, crying out as she did when vexed. Hank headed not for me, but for the kitchen, saying, "I'd better open this over the sink in case it bubbles over."

At least I wanted it this time; I wanted the happy ending and violins playing in the background. I wasn't clutching my throat and running toward the bathroom to hide. As we toasted our glasses with the French champagne, I kept thinking of the movie scenario, the one that kept running in my head.

I tried to stay present with Hank, and not escape to our movie-self counterparts, but the film kept running in my head, more vivid and alive than this real life scene.

"Mmmmm. This tastes wonderful, the best ever," I said to keep myself in the real world. The bubbles tickled me, and I did love the taste.

"Merry Christmas. It's great to be with you. I wish you great holidays," he said with a lift of the wine glass.

He left at eleven, insisting on leaving the champagne with me. I tried to say it as he shrugged on his brown coat. My vocal chords vibrated with the words I wanted to say.

"Hank," I said as my courage plummeted.

"Yes?" He stood calmly, expectant, his green eyes alert.

"I just wanted to say something." My throat tightened noticeably.

"Go ahead, dear."

His hand gripped the door knob and fear filled my heart.

"Have a great Christmas," I said, unable to complete my mission.

"You, too." He stuck out his hand and we shook awkwardly. In a moment he was gone.

"That wasn't the Hollywood version," I told Tricksie later, when she had resumed her campaign to remove all the tree ornaments.

"I wanted to ask him to stay. Instead I say 'Have a great Christmas.' What kind of a passionate beginning is that?"

Tricksie stopped mauling a soft brown bear ornament just long enough to look at me and say, "Mah." I think in cat language that means "better than you think."

I lit every last candle in my house, turned off the lights, and sipped at the delightful champagne bubbles that erased the cares of the world.

Christmas carols filled any remaining void, sung by Barbra Streisand, Julie Andrews, Mariah Carey, and many more.

That hour of complete contentment rushed by, and the next time I looked at my watch, it was 12:15 a.m. Christmas day. Despite loyalties to Circle and Wiccans, it still felt special.

"Merry Christmas, Trickster," I said, picking up the sleeping fur ball, depositing a noisy kiss on her cat fur.

I felt her rough pink tongue on my hand, and I felt loved.

"This is altogether the nicest Christmas I can remember," I told her as I reluctantly blew out candles and unplugged the tree lights and carried her back toward our bedroom.

* * *

Candles again lit the room, but this time the upstairs front room at Friend's Meeting House. I'd come a little late, though the road had been clear—past the middle of January and only a few inches of snow here and there. I was thankful for the dry highway, for safe navigation to the other side of town.

"You're just in time, Moonbeam." Isis embraced me. She was wearing tie-dyed shirt and pants, shades of shocking blue, purple, orange, and yellow.

I counted twelve of us, a great turnout for a full moon ritual in January. The ladies sat around the central altar cloth where most of the candles flamed. A few shed light from the fireplace mantel.

Isis and I slid into place in our circle.

"I know I scheduled kundalini yoga for this week," Isis said, "but you probably received my e-mail about the problem plaguing Circle for several months now. I want to talk about that tonight." She explained about Flo's disappearance from the group, and her confrontation with Flo that preceded that. She explained our efforts to reach her.

"But it just sounds like Flo got mad and left. What makes you think there's any foul play involved?" Genevieve asked.

Isis explained about our tarot spread findings, about our strong sense of danger. Something had gone deadly wrong.

"It doesn't make sense that Flo quit her job, either, unless it was a coincidence. Why would she quit her job if she was mad at us?" I said.

"I have another piece of evidence, though it doesn't clear anything up. Today I received a note from Flo," Isis said.

I gazed at her, startled. She produced a small, yellow ruled sheet of paper. She cleared her throat and read clearly to us.

"Isis, Queen of Sheba,

I am very happy now, in a place where I am loved and appreciated. My new friends have been much kinder than you and your mealy-mouthed woman friends.

Your stupid attempts at being witches make me laugh. This group has power, real power, and makes you all look like little girls playing tea party.

I haven't forgotten your ugliness and you can be sure you will be repaid in kind.

Flo Pohaski

"Before any of you speak up and say this just proves that Flo is mad at me and us, let me explain something. When I picked this out of the pile of mail, I felt nauseated. My energy drained out of me, and I felt sick. Then I opened it, and realized it came from Flo.

"This isn't what it seems to be. I don't know what this means, but I'd be cautious to label it." Isis passed the note to Gretchen next to her and sat back cross-legged.

"What about the postmark? Could you find out where she mailed this?" Gretchen asked.

"I left that at home. It was so faint I couldn't read it."

"All of this is beyond me," Diana said, a young woman with short, bouncy dark hair. "Here we are trying to honor Mother Earth and each other. I don't understand this Flo business at all. We all tried to be nice to her, but no matter how hard we tried, she only had negative things to say. She whined and cried and made a general nuisance of herself. Like a Flo plague.

"There was nothing normal about her being amongst us. Flo was always a dark force amongst our creations of light. I wonder if historically Flo was something to us."

"You mean back in time? Like in another lifetime?" Gretchen asked.

"That's exactly what I mean," Diana said.

"That could be true," Isis said. "We can meditate and try to unearth some ideas, but I have an even better thought. Carol Abel has done psychic readings for me. Her information was dead on, and she helped me. I could ask her to join us to unveil the past and present."

We talked as the candles dripped and shortened, and all agreed that Carol Abel might help us unravel the mystery. The younger ladies still seemed unconcerned about Flo, as if nothing had happened. But Isis, the older ladies, and I nodded toward each other knowingly.

Still, our session somehow ended early, so we girls proceeded to make the best of the remaining minutes.

"I'll let you know when and if Carol can join us. Since we have some time, I thought we could do a part of the kundalini yoga," Isis said.

Heads nodded around the circle, and no one got up to leave.

"Everybody lie on your back with legs outstretched before you. This one is a great toner for the abdominal muscles."

Groans filled the room.

"Isis, Queen of Kundalini," someone shouted, and we chanted it until the queen began our abdominal toning with great enthusiasm and no mercy.

Chapter 9

The next day, I wheeled into the K-Mart parking lot intent on an emergency mission. I'd run out of furnace filters, a deadly blunder now that winter's icy fingers clutched at us. The wind blew sharply, blasting small, dry snowflakes into my face. The old filter looked gruesome; it was dark and furry, like it needed a name and a collar. A few cars dotted the huge, weathered macadam lot. This would be a quick dash in and out, then on to work.

What mystifies me is that I always made these quick trips after work, not before. So today I changed my routine and the course of my life at the same time. And K-Mart provided the exotic setting, open twenty-four hours of every day, eternally vigilant of consumers' needs.

I flew down a main aisle beside electronics when I perceived movement out of the corner of my eye, but a millisecond too late to change my course.

We collided instantaneously, with a sickening loud thud. Searing, hot pain flashed through my left side, especially my head, and I heard a few groans as I sensed a tall, slender figure next to me.

"What happened?" he said, and put a hand on my shoulder after he dusted off his suit jacket. His dark eyes peered into me beneath short black hair and I felt as if he already knew all my secrets. A cell phone dangled from his other hand. "You hurt?"

"Can't tell. I don't see any blood. See any blood?" Maybe I should have mentioned the throbbing in my head.

He shook his head and plastered his cell phone back onto his ear, talking loudly.

Volatile anger bordering on rage consumed me, and in this instant this man became my mortal enemy.

"Excuse me," I said louder than his phone voice, jarring my aching head.

He turned his back and ignored me. Big mistake.

I should have just walked off, but the anger gave me jet propulsion and courage to speak. I got right in his face and said, "Turn that thing off before I get the store manager."

He looked totally annoyed, which pleased me.

"I'll get back to you, Mike," he said, and flicked off his phone. "Now what is going on? I thought you were all right."

"I didn't know you were talking on your cell phone. Do you realize how many accidents those things cause? You weren't paying attention to where you were."

"I'm sorry," he said, but he looked more vexed than repentant. "I didn't mean to cause an accident, but you were moving pretty fast, lady. I feel banged up myself. I have friends who are lawyers."

"And I've never collided in K-Mart before. I always move this fast. When you talk on that cell phone continuously throughout the day, you are never in the present moment. So you are never fully alive. You do all of society a big disservice, especially yourself. And I'm not afraid of your lawyers."

He eyed me with awakening interest.

"You're not just anybody, are you?" he asked, picking his words carefully.

"I'm pretty ordinary, normal as the next person." I felt suddenly on the defensive as the adrenalin seeped out of my system.

His slight smile disarmed me, and he filed the phone inside his navy suit jacket.

"Well, maybe not normal," I said. "I meditate, you know."

"Are you some kind of New Age 'Let the sunshine in' person?" His black eyes examined me as if he'd cornered some new exotic breed of bird.

I ruffled my plumage.

"I've been studying the metaphysical world for several years now. It's more of a hobby than anything." I didn't intend to be more specific than that. "Besides, I have to go to work now or I'll be late."

"Oh, no, lovely lady—you've gotten my attention. It's not over yet. How can I reach you?" He leaned toward me, and I caught a whiff of some expensive men's cologne. It wasn't Old Spice.

"Reach me?" For what?

"Telephone number, whatever. I might want to talk to you some more. Not might, more like definitely." He pulled a business card and pen out of a pocket.

"Just give me your card, and I'll call you." Somehow, I didn't think he'd fall for it.

He handed me his card to my relief, then pulled another out of his pocket.

"You won't call me, so how about some number where I can reach you? You'd better hurry or you'll be late for work. By the way, where do you work?"

"Ruthie's Diner," I said, then clamped a hand over my betraying lips.

"On Steubenville Pike?" I nodded, feeling doubly doomed. He brightened considerably. "That's fine, then. I'll contact you there. What's your name, dear?"

"Stephanie. Just plain Stephanie, like Cher or Jewel. You're Alexander Demetrius," I said as I read his card on expensive paper.

"At your service," he said and bowed low. "Go to work, and I'll talk to you later. I'll use my home phone. I'd say I was sorry about the bump, but everything has its time and purpose."

"Now you sound like the New Age person," I said as I backed away.

He shrugged his tailored shoulders as I turned and accelerated, moving faster than before our head-on collision. I jumped behind the wheel of the Escort and accelerated down the hill before I even remembered the furnace filters.

Furnace filters didn't seem like such an emergency any more. I'd have to go back later, when I had more time and when I understood why Alexander Demetrius had looked so fascinating and desirable in K-Mart.

* * *

I sat across from him in the unfamiliar surroundings feeling faint. I tried to breathe deeply, but smoke kept wafting my way. We sat in non-smoking in the zone just beyond smoking, never a good choice for me.

"Are you sure this is a good idea?" I asked him, absorbing the sterile atmosphere, the strange faces.

"I hope so. I don't think it's a bad idea, merely an attempt to move us along," Hank said. He shifted in our booth and looked handsome in purple shirt and gray corduroys.

"So we've come here to Ritter's Diner in Bloomfield to change our place of meeting, but not change it too much. In other words, we're still in a diner."

"It does seem odd, I admit, but we can't stay stuck in that diner—I mean Ruthie's. I want more if it's possible." Hank stirred a cup of coffee, making that comforting clinking sound with the spoon.

"So does this mean we'll be meeting at diners all over Pittsburgh, maybe all over the state and country?"

His face lit up from a smile deep within. "I suppose we could, but that's not really what I had in mind."

I wanted to ask him what he had in mind, but I couldn't get the words out.

He reached across the table and held my hands.

"I just feel so comfortable with you, Stephanie, right from the first day you poured me a cup of coffee and smiled. I felt special with you, and you listened deeply to the things I said.

"I've always felt drawn to you, but we can leave it the way it is. I can continue as your customer. I don't want it that way because I always dreamed we'd spend some time together.

"I guess I need to know what you think. Whatever you say, I'll accept."

Hank looked more alluring than ever—handsome and solid and caring. I wasn't sure if the thumping of my heart was from fear or excitement.

"You know it's hard for me to talk of these things," I started.

"I know." He leaned forward with sincerity blazing in his green eyes.

"I'm blanking out."

"This diner is open twenty-four hours, so I'll wait until you're ready."

"You know it's not because I don't like you. I like you very much and look forward to seeing you."

"I know." His voice was kind and reassuring.

"I was married once a long time ago, and only briefly. I felt trapped and unhappy. Honestly, Hank, I rarely get involved with men."

"But I'm no mortal man. I'm a faithful customer, and we've been talking together for three years now."

“Part of me wants to reach out to you. You don’t need to worry about that. I’ve always been attracted to you. But there’s this other part of me that has never been able to do it. And then if it doesn’t work you’ll shift over to Rosemary’s station and I’ll have to look at you and be heartbroken.”

“Actually, I’d probably switch to that new girl’s section—Connie.”

We burst out laughing together.

“We’ll go slowly, as slowly as you like if only you want to try it with me. I need to know if that’s what you want, too.”

“Here we go getting serious again. Yes, I want to try even though I’m terrified and I have a nice, decent, comfortable life already. I can’t guarantee we won’t end up back in Ruthie’s part of the time, because I freeze up sometimes.

“The answer is yes. Yes, I want to try.

Chapter 10

The ritual room quieted to silence, a miracle in itself, as Circle met at Isis's house. Thirteen of us sat cross-legged around the altar cloth set with pink and purple candles. We waited in anticipation of a message, of enlightenment. We waited in hopes of word of Flo, for whatever Spirit offered tonight. Another full moon, well into February, brought no word of her, only plummeting temperatures, slippery roads, and shovels full of snow.

Across from me sat Isis in a golden, shimmering pants outfit. She spoke briefly with a thin, blonde woman beside her, then stood up. Incense burning on the altar reached my nostrils, and the sweet scent of jasmine filled my being.

I nearly trembled in anticipation of something, I didn't know what. Would we receive word of Flo? Would Spirit speak to me? My visions had flooded my mind, and I wondered if another was coming tonight. I felt a shiver up and down my spine as that face filled my memory, the man with the loving eyes. I often thought of him and tried to understand that message.

"We will be working tonight as a group to locate Flo Pohaski, so our regular ritual will be held later. Carol Abel has agreed to help us."

Isis turned to the petite lady with the short blonde, layered hair and extended a hand.

"Carol is a medium, psychic, and an ordained minister. We met at Mandala Books, where we both do readings. Her work has helped me with insights into my life and fresh approaches to old dilemmas.

"She has graciously offered to donate her time and gifts tonight to help us. At the end of our session she would also be glad to answer a few personal questions. I turn our meeting over to you, Carol. Thanks for coming," Isis said, whose purple glitter nail polish matched the altar cloth.

We clapped with enthusiasm as Carol rose, showing off her long, maroon velour dress and cross of moonstone around her neck. A pretty, delicate-looking woman of forty, she had a few extra wrinkles on her face that spoke of personal hardship.

"I want to thank you all for asking me to come. The energy of this group is wonderful—very warm. Yet I feel power here, too, and I can sense each of you is on a path of growth. I want to get down to business so we'll have time for a few questions at the end.

"I understand you're missing a Circle member, that there were ugly words, but you still suspect foul play. She vanished, leaving only a nasty note behind. Let's do a meditation first to raise our vibrational rate," Carol said.

She led us in a meditation as we visualized Flo and surrounded her with light. We called upon angels to assist her in whatever her mission and to help us locate the truth about her. All in all, it was a powerful meditation, and by the time Carol asked us to open our eyes, I felt as if I'd come back from a faraway place.

I looked around our magical circle and noticed others stretching or rubbing their eyes. I decided to believe whatever Carol had to say.

She waited until we all were back and then spoke with quiet confidence. "I got a sense of Flo during the meditation. Isis told me Flo complained and was negative. By the way, you need not feed information to a psychic. We do as well or better with an empty slate.

"I sense even more than that. Flo was much more than any of you realized. She represented an energy to this group, a destructive force, a force of darkness.

"I see dark clouds. This darkness also extended back into past lives. I feel in a past life, Flo hurt you all somehow. I'm not sure what happened then, but Flo has returned to haunt you in a much less potent form this time.

"I sense jealousy here. She felt inferior to you all. She never felt she was a part of this group." Carol sat upright, her eyes open, but dreamy.

"What about the present with Flo? What is going on with her now?" Isis asked.

Carol hesitated a minute. "I'm getting faded images, nothing clear, mostly impressions. She trusts the wrong people because of her jealousy and hurt, and she's so filled with hatred that she can't make good judgments.

"This may be some karmic debt she's chosen to repay. In other words, she hurt this group, so another group will take her life."

Carol stopped and turned even paler under her makeup, and I held my breath. Isis looked rattled.

"I'm not sure where that came from," Carol said, sitting up even taller so her black granny boots showed. "Maybe that's not true."

"Can you establish where Flo is right now?" Isis asked.

"It's all fuzzy. Others surround her, and in this group Flo is the enlightened one. They are drawn to her, but they destroy all they touch. Dark, troubled souls surround Flo. But I can't see where she is, maybe nearby. I can't tell who these people are or where they have her."

"You think she might be in the city?" I asked.

"Maybe, maybe not. I have no strong sense of location. I'm sorry, I'm afraid I'm not being very helpful."

"No, Carol, you're being extremely helpful. We should have called on you weeks ago. You're giving us new information, and more than we've been able to gather," Isis said.

Carol smiled and nodded. "One last thing, ladies. I see flames, hear loud crackling, feel tremendous heat, smell strong smoke. What do flames mean, I wonder?"

"The Burning Times," several of us intoned together, like a long-forgotten chant.

"Burning witches? Like in medieval times when innocents were denounced and torched?" Carol asked, the light of understanding in her eyes.

"That was a chilling, evil period. I don't even like to think of it." Isis shivered, and I felt myself involuntarily shivering, too.

"Something about flames or the Burning Times," Carol said. "My guides aren't giving me any more information."

"What about the part earlier when you said the group would kill Flo? Is she dead now?" Diana asked.

Carol paused for several minutes. "Good question. I asked my guides, and I'm getting confusing information. I tried to contact her in the spirit world, but I got no response. I don't think you can find her or change the course of events. Maybe you could, but Flo has determined her own fate. She's teaching herself some lesson."

"So you don't think we should go to the police and tell them Flo is missing and our spirit guides warned us she's in mortal danger?" Isis asked with a Mona Lisa smile.

"I wish we could," Carol said, her face serious. "We might save her life. Does anyone want to say a prayer? That's about all we can do at this point."

We held hands in our circle. Diana prayed, then Jennifer, both heartfelt prayers asking for Flo's deliverance from harm. When they finished, I sat up straight, not feeling the stiffness in my legs from sitting on the floor. My pulse quickened, and I realized this part of our evening was what I waited for with excitement.

All around our group, the faces mirrored expectancy. Carol would give us messages.

"Now for the happy part of our program tonight. I hope to give each one of you a personal message from Spirit," Carol said, commanding our full attention. "Who would like a message? Just raise your hands or speak up and ask a question."

"What about my living quarters?" Diana asked.

"You're looking for a house to buy." Diana nodded her head. "I see another part of town, even though you've been looking in your immediate area. Don't worry about which direction to turn—the way will be shown you.

"The grounds are lovely, but you won't know that until spring. Lovely flowers and bushes flourish in a secluded back yard amidst several statues and a fountain."

"But can we afford all that?" Diana blurted out.

Carol laughed. "My guides tell me this house is right within your price range. The feeling I get is of love and growth and understanding. A place to retreat from the world. Another question from someone else?"

Carol talked and we all listened, especially the petitioner, and I found the work fascinating. I thought about asking a question, but I felt timid, and our session was winding down. Nearly everyone else had asked for information. I wanted to ask about Hank, but didn't want my love life exposed in public.

"I have a message for you," Carol said, turning to me.

"Message? Me?" I looked around for someone else.

"Yes, you," Carol said, laughing. "Your name is Stephanie, isn't it?"

"How did you know?" I was amazed.

"We went around and said our names earlier."

I heard snorts around our circle.

"Anyway, the message is love is headed your way, but it may not turn out the way you expect. The ways of the soul are strange," Carol said.

"Is it someone I know?" I said, embarrassed, yet wanting to know more.

"You deserve all the love and care in the world, Stephanie. You've been keeping to yourself, locked away. Fear has kept you in this small place where love cannot blossom or grow.

"Yes, I think you know this man. I can't tell you any more except that this will be better than you ever expected. You will grow in this new atmosphere, feel at home."

"What's his name?" I asked.

Carol crinkled her pretty face. "I'm bad at names. I don't hear them right, I guess. More important than the name is the feeling you get when you are with him."

"Thanks, Carol," I said, feeling weak. My dreams of romance were far back in the past. Even though Hank wanted more, I secretly thought our efforts were doomed. This message served as a revelation to me.

After a few words from Isis, Circle was finished for this week. Isis grabbed me and I nearly cried on her shoulder, for the session had been stressful, especially my personal message.

"She probably just meant the cat," I said in a strangled voice.

"You'll just have to see, my friend. But I don't think she meant that." Isis wiggled her eyebrows, and I felt laughter bubbling up and bursting through my fears.

Chapter 11

"Tricksie, Tricksie, where are you?" I called from my bed, my eyes barely open. I felt sweaty, and my chest heaved with ragged breathing.

"Mah," came clearly from the comforter thrown back, concealing her. She lay curled up near my chest right beside me. I reached for her as a child might reach for a teddy bear. I wanted to squeeze her tightly to me, but instead patted her soundly.

"Bad dream, Tricksie," I said, putting my face to her silken side. "Make it better, please." I remembered our Circle meeting from last night, which grounded me to earth.

Outside, a cardinal song erupted melodious and clear from the tall oak beyond my window. I caught a streak of red as he winged onward, yet his eternal optimism failed to cheer me.

I felt awful. Part of me remained in the dream world. The images made me shiver and pull closer to my companion.

I'd been running in the dream. I ran away, trying to escape certain death. It was fall and I wore a rough dress, and I should have been cold, but the numbness felt good.

I was numb with cold, numb with fear. Something unspeakable had happened. I had to keep running or I'd be taken, too.

In my heart I knew I couldn't outrun my fate. It was all sealed up, no matter what I did.

Then there were flames all around me, and the numb cold and searing heat mixed together and a face hung large high above me.

It was Flo's face, but it wasn't her face, and it was shining like a full moon with contorted features above the flames. I saw a dark figure in the distance, pacing in a long cassock. I couldn't see his face, yet I knew him somehow.

Flo laughed now, an unpleasant, rough laugh that had no joy in it. Somehow her laughter made me more uncomfortable than the flames. But I couldn't breathe now, and that's when I woke up, feeling suffocated.

I'd calmed down, thanks to Tricksie, and so I could face the real world. Kissing her furry head, I swung out of bed and listened to another cardinal in the tree.

"It's spring," I whispered to my cat, though the vernal equinox was a month away. "Spring is coming. Nothing to worry about."

We burst out onto my small back porch and I felt the life-giving caress of the sun. Looking down, I almost expected to see the rough dress of my dream, but my short red night shirt was still there.

Tricksie rubbed at my ankles, and I inhaled deeply of this day. Yes, it felt like spring had arrived. Out here my dream didn't seem important or particularly frightening.

Yet thoughts of my dream continued to haunt me throughout the day as I did household chores, then drove to Ruthie's Diner for the evening shift.

I spied his Bronco parked in front before I slid into the rear of the lot. He was early tonight. I could feel tension building in my chest and my heart thumped in some odd rhythm.

I slipped in the back and found a black apron to tie over my cherry blouse and black pants. We all wore different color blouses to vary the look. Though some of the girls wore skirts, I always wore pants. They just suited me better.

"Hank was asking about you," Rosemary said, appearing out of nowhere.

I jumped. "You scared me. Everything scares me today."

"What is it, Steph? You look like you just saw a ghost."

"Something from my past, maybe. I had a wild dream about death and destruction that seemed real. I'm still waiting for the bad guys to come and get me." I twirled a strand of hair that had escaped my ponytail.

"Oh, my." Rosemary was not often speechless.

"I see Hank is here early," I observed to change the subject, unsure that Hank was such a safe subject after all.

"He's been here half an hour. He thought you started earlier. Everything all right there? And if it's not, you don't have to answer." She sounded edgy.

"It's all right. Did I tell you that Hank and I had dinner at Ritter's Diner last month? I enjoyed his company, but Ritter's doesn't begin to compare with Ruthie's. For one thing, the service was very slow."

"Should have taken your apron along."

"I'd have been more comfortable that way. Not that I was that uncomfortable. Actually, I had a pretty good time." I hadn't admitted that to myself until I heard me say it.

"Glad to hear it. You two have a lot in common. And you've spent more time together than some married couples. I'd better get back out there." Rosemary blew me a kiss and disappeared, leaving me to ponder what Hank and I had in common.

We both spent time at Ruthie's Diner?

I inhaled big breaths to take the edge off the excitement I felt at seeing Hank again. Life at the diner had been peaceful—never dull, though. There were enough characters who strolled through the doors to make every day interesting.

I checked my makeup in the small bathroom mirror, then wondered why I was fussing about my looks. What was wrong with me? I rarely worried about what I looked like. This man-attraction thing always made me more insecure than ever.

He sat right up at the counter beaming at me, as if he knew exactly when I'd arrive. I resisted an impulse to breeze right past him.

"Hello, Hank. Can I get anything for you?" Even to me, the words sounded stiff, formal.

"Since you just got here, I guess you can't sit and talk." I knew he wanted me to contradict him.

"It's pretty quiet, Hank. I can go around and check everyone, then grab a few minutes with you. If anyone new comes into my section, I'll just jump up."

He nodded, and his green eyes shone brightly, like the green of a stop light beckoning me to "go, go, go" to him. They drew me in, and I'd have been mesmerized if I didn't have to check my tables.

I surveyed my station, refilled coffee and drinks, removed some plates, and delivered key lime pie to the Wright brothers. It seemed to take forever, but it must not have, for Hank was still there when I returned.

"You're early today," I said and dropped onto the stool beside him. He'd put his briefcase on it to hold it for me.

"I wanted to see you before I go. I'm going away for a week, could be longer. I didn't want you to think I was running out on you." He stared into his coffee cup like it was a crystal ball.

I sipped at my cup of decaf to stall. I wondered if he really was running away from our situation.

"I'm glad you stopped to tell me. I might have taken it personally otherwise. Am I allowed to ask where you're going?"

He licked his lips and shifted on his stool. I thought he looked handsome even when fidgeting.

"I have family business to take care of, so I'm taking vacation." He wiggled more on his stool. "It's not the way I care to spend vacation time, but family obligations call."

"So you're the dutiful family member. You're not spending the week away as a scholar and professor?"

"This time I wish I were. I'm seriously thinking about signing up for some study sessions in a foreign location."

"Where will you be this time? I have to go soon." I spoke the words softly, calmly.

"I'll be doing some traveling. I'm not certain where all I'll be, but unfortunately, I'll be out of town most of the time."

"Then I'll miss you," I said, though a part of me felt relief.

"I do care about you. I feel rotten about deserting you right now. Please forgive me. You're so important to me, and I don't want to jeopardize our future."

The smile froze on my face as I felt the butterflies in my midsection transform into a horde of hornets.

He sensed my distress and put a warm hand on mine.

"I seem to be making this muddle into a worse mess. Forgive me," he said.

I smiled and put a hand on his arm as I stood up.

"I understand. Please be careful on your trip. Tell Granny I said yoo-hoo." I gave him a carefully placed kiss on the cheek.

"I'll be going, too, Steph. Thanks for talking to me."

"Call me when you get back."

"I don't have your number."

"Yes, you do."

"Right. I forgot. I'll call. I'll check in when I can." His words sounded strangely unconvincing.

The diner doors opened, admitting a tall, thin man with black straight hair. He stepped to the side, admiring the cakes and pies in the revolving showcase. Hank, gaze downward, strode right out of the diner.

The black-haired man stared at me, a smile slowly lighting his features.

"So you really do work here," he said in wonder.

"Hello, Alex," I said.

Chapter 12

A fluttering in my chest perplexed and surprised me as I realized how happy I was to see him. I tried to restrain my greeting.

"You found me," I said, feeling awkward.

He didn't seem to care. "I've been thinking about you. What I've been thinking doesn't fit in with this diner atmosphere."

He sounded serious, and I caught my breath. My heart continued its acrobatics.

"What did you have in mind, Alex?"

"Who was that guy you were talking to? I just caught it out of the corner of my eye. It looked intense."

So he was perceptive as well as handsome. "They're all customers in here, but he's a friend as well. Not that I need to answer that."

His eyes lit up briefly. "It really doesn't matter—curiosity, that was all. Listen, I'm still in the midst of some deals, and you look like you're busy. Later on, I should have some free time. What time do you get off work?"

"Is this a trick question?" I paused and considered. "Maybe a little after eleven."

"That's perfect. I'll pick you up when you're done."

"I don't know. I'd rather try it some time when I can relax and get ready. I'll smell like pies, cakes, and French fries." I felt anxious, yet underneath it all my motor raced.

"I'd like to see you tonight so you can lecture me some more about my cell phone. I need to learn about authoritative women. My past history mostly covers submissive ones."

"I don't know you."

"Hey, Stephanie, how about some more coffee?" I heard from halfway across the room. Wilbur and Orville swung their coffee mugs in the air to salute me. I felt a wave of guilt that I was neglecting my customers. I needed to decide and get back to work, at least that's what I told myself.

I let my gut make the choice.

"Come a little after eleven and I'll go with you. But I can't stay out late."

"Why not? That's about the time I get started."

"Never mind. An hour or two tonight—that's all I have to offer. Take it or leave it." I folded my arms and tried to look tough.

"I love the way you command me, darling. I'll be back later." He turned and breezed out as casually as he'd slipped in.

I quickly checked my tables, refilled drinks, and delivered pie to a few customers. Alex had left behind an aftermath of jumbled feelings. I quickly slipped out the back, where I was greeted by sun, spring, and bird song. Yet all that glory was wasted on me. My vision could only see inward.

Though I was a mass of feelings, I didn't know what I felt.

Why am I going out tonight with Alex? Why would I want to see him? I've only just begun with Hank. Hank is true, blue, and I trust him.

With a sick sensation, I wondered if Alex hadn't arrived at this moment in time so I could once again avoid commitment. After all, I'd lived this way all my adult life.

I realized I did have hopes and dreams for Hank and me. I'd tried to put it out of my head and heart, but it was definitely there. Maybe there was hope after all.

As for Alex, I'd have to play that by ear. One thing I'd felt, but hadn't put into words yet—that I'd known him before—a tiny inkling that we'd met before, but I couldn't place him. Maybe soon I'd remember.

With a sigh, I looked around me, then opened the back door to the diner.

Back to work, Steph. Better stick to work and forget about romance.

* * *

Yet a feeling of unreality persisted throughout the evening as I coasted through my shift, relying on years of reflexes as a waitress.

"Stephanie, where are you? You aren't yourself tonight. Your head is way up in the clouds somewhere." Fred, a white-haired gentleman, was one of my evening regulars.

"Hush, Fred. Stephanie's allowed to be a little dreamy once in a while," said Alma, his matching white-haired wife. They were always concerned about me.

"I'm all right, you two. Can't get away with anything around here, can I?" I flashed my "family" a brilliant smile.

As the evening drifted on, I changed my mind about the date with Alex. I desperately wanted to cancel it, but I'd left his business card with the phone number at home.

When he strolled in the door at eleven, looking tall and elegant in his black suit and red silk tie, all my speeches froze in my throat.

He looked absolutely wonderful.

Then he smiled at me.

Oh, sweet heaven—I was filled with joy.

I have a two-inch lead crystal ball hanging in my house. It's faceted all over, and when the light hits it, it glitters in great beauty with rainbow colors. So Alex looked now—utterly fascinating. His smile glittered, and my resolutions faded away in his energies and physical presence.

"Hello, gorgeous," he said as I took off my apron.

"You look all right yourself. I'll be ready in a minute. Would you like a cup of coffee?"

"Sure. Black." He sat at the counter as if he owned it, but he looked out of place. Ruthie's may have never known such elegance before.

I poured his coffee, then stepped into the back, making last-ditch efforts to beautify myself in the bathroom. After five minutes, I gave up. My cherry short-sleeve shirt and black work pants would have to do. Makeup could only do so much. I looked tired and pale.

"I'm ready," I said, facing Alex from the opposite side of the counter.

"You look wonderful. Let's get out of here," he said, pulling bills out of one pocket.

"The coffee's on the house."

"In that case, I should have come in earlier and had dinner. The food looks good, especially the cakes and pies on display there," he said, pointing to the glass case.

"Ruthie's quite a cook."

"I have to admit, today was the first I ever came in here. I entertain a lot for business purposes, so the atmosphere is usually pretty posh."

"Our customers can relate better to homey than posh." I was feeling out of my element already.

"So where are we headed tonight for our fantasy date in wonderland?" Alex took my arm and steered me out the door and into the parking lot. He stopped beside a black sport utility vehicle. The night was frigid, yet clear, the stars overhead poignant with light.

"What is this?" I asked, nodding toward the vehicle. In the lit-up parking lot it looked like a combination hearse and black bus.

"What do you mean by that? This is the latest in high tech driving. It's a recreational vehicle, but I use it for all my business driving."

I walked around it, noting the markings.

"It's a Cadillac. So you're combining the elegance of a luxury vehicle with the ruggedness of a sport model. Very interesting."

"Image is important in my work. You can't be too concerned about image."

"You've never told me what you do. What is your work, Alex?" I barely knew this man, and here I was escaping into the night with him.

"Get in. We'll talk on the way."

I still felt breathless around him, and it seemed all right to be with him—comfortable in some respects, yet exciting, too.

"I'm a developer," he said as he turned down the road. The interior of the vehicle was beige plush.

"Photographs?"

He wrinkled his face. "No—land. Shopping malls. That sort of thing. You're funny, Steph."

"I do exist in my own little world here at the diner and at home with my cat. I'm not a very worldly person. I live just a few miles from the heart of downtown Pittsburgh, yet I'm not a part of it."

"You're better off that way. I'm sure you have a wholesome way of life."

"How about you? Do you have a wholesome way of life?"

He laughed as he steered us into the darkness.

"I can't ever remember being wholesome, not even as a child. I'm given to excesses: drink too much, eat the wrong food, take on as many sexual partners as I can find—women, that is."

I sat and digested this information.

"Where are we going?" I asked.

"You'll see. I think you'll like this. Are you hungry? Should I buy you something to eat?"

"I don't usually eat after work. I eat something during my shift. But thank you, anyway."

Part of me wondered why I was going into the night with this complete stranger who admitted to being a man of excesses. Was there something wrong with me?

Of course there was, but this was in addition to that. I idly wondered if I was in some danger, but it didn't feel that way. My instincts usually kept me safe.

"Have we met before, Stephanie?" he said so suddenly that I jumped.

"What makes you ask that?"

"Ever since we ran into each other in K-Mart, I've had this haunting feeling that I know you. Yet I can't remember meeting you before."

"I know. I've felt that way, too, but we don't exactly circulate in the same social circles."

"Maybe I'll remember. I hardly ever forget a face, or a name, for that matter. Your name wasn't at all familiar to me."

"We'll figure it out," I said hopefully, but a part of me didn't believe we would.

"We're here," he announced as he wheeled into a parking lot.

I smiled as I began to understand our destination.

"It's time you learned a little bit about the city," he said after he opened my door. "All of this is yours to savor, my lady."

He gently kissed my hand before helping me out of the Cadillac.

The night felt young.

Chapter 13

"I hardly ever come here," I said, still recovering from my continental kiss. "I bet I haven't been here in five years."

"I have to admit, I come here pretty often to do business."

"Two different worlds," I said.

We walked toward the river, which we could see from beside his vehicle. I instantly caught the magic of the place. As a backdrop to this cold, clear evening, the lights of the city dominated our view. The high-rise buildings of the city, the Golden Triangle, lay across the river from us. Our shoes crunched on the snow-crusted ground.

We stood across the Monongahela River at Station Square, a popular area for shopping and dining. The old P & LE railroad station had been converted long ago into a restaurant and bar. Another larger building housed shops and restaurants.

"Do you want to try a restaurant? We could go to the Gandy Dancer," he said.

"Oh, no. And miss this place?" I motioned toward the river and city. He stared at the same scene that enchanted me.

"I guess I don't see it anymore," he said, wrinkling his brow.

"Can we sit out here?" Glad for our winter coats, I pointed to a bench facing the river.

"Certainly, my lady. Anywhere at all. Would you like to get drinks and bring them out here?"

"I don't drink much, Alex. We can go in and get you a drink."

He frowned.

"Not necessary. I'll just enjoy the evening and your excellent company." He dusted off the bench and looked into my eyes deliberately just as we sat on it. "I didn't know you were into all this natural stuff."

"You don't know me at all. We crashed into each other once. That's our history. And yet," I said and stopped.

"And yet you feel tremendously attracted to me as if something occurred between us somewhere, somehow before."

"I admit I'm attracted. You can use whatever qualifier you want. But that feeling of familiarity persists."

"I know," he said simply. He sat up against me. Where our thighs touched, I felt electricity.

"You speak like an educated person. Have you done work other than waitressing?"

"I have a degree in journalism, but I found waitress work suited me best. It's straightforward and honest work."

"So you're frittering your days away as a waitress, letting life pass you by?"

I hesitated a minute, not wanting to offend this man. Somehow, I didn't find his comment abrasive.

"I'm going to get serious, so please forgive me. I've always lived a life of service to others, and that is my way. I believe to become enlightened one must pursue that path. As I serve others, I serve myself. That positive, nurturing energy cycles back to me.

"Does any of this make sense to you?"

His fixed smile and blank stare answered my question. I knew he couldn't understand what I was telling him.

"But wouldn't you rather be a freelance writer than hoist burgers and French fries? Wouldn't you rather lead an exciting life meeting fascinating people and exploring interesting subjects?" His face wore a puzzled look.

Alex, Alex, how can I ever explain this to you? I sensed he was world-weary, jaded by time and excessive experiences.

"My days are exciting in their own quiet little way. That's my secret to a fulfilling life—get excited about all the small moments in one's day.

"For instance, I heard a cardinal this morning and saw him in the huge oak tree behind my house. His song filled my heart with joy. Not only that, but the oak tree is magnificent. He's an elderly gentleman with lots of charisma and holes for the squirrels and woodland creatures."

Alex clasped his hands together.

"You really are a back-to-nature person, aren't you?" he said.

"I've always loved the animals and creatures, even the trees and plants, the wind and rain. It's not like I go camping or anything like that. I just feel a strong connection with the natural world—God's creation."

I thought about my newly-discovered Circle friends, my rituals with the witches, but decided to limit my sharing for now. I didn't know this man.

"I can't relate to what you're saying. I don't understand it. I spend my days in the Cadillac, in expensive restaurants, in bars, and in hotel rooms. I don't get this nature worship routine. Maybe it's because I'm an atheist."

Was there an envious gleam in his eye, a far-away look that lusted for what I had? I imagined I sensed those things in him, just for a minute.

"We don't have much in common," I observed, looking out at the beauty of the Golden Triangle. The river water flowed on past us and on beyond.

Before he could reply, I switched subjects. "This is the area's energetic center, you know."

"Because of the city, the buildings?" he asked.

"Not at all. Hundreds and thousands of years ago it was the same. It's because of the rivers."

"So these three rivers are powerful," he said.

"That's it. They form a strong energy vortex because of the river energy, especially where the Mon and the Allegheny merge to form the Ohio River."

"This isn't at all what I expected. I thought we'd have this exciting, romantic night out, share some drinks and laughs, maybe sleep together," Alex said.

"Are you disappointed?"

He studied the opposite shore.

"Maybe not. Maybe those exciting evenings haven't been all that exciting lately. They were getting a bit routine. I'm very good at seducing women," he said matter-of-factly.

"That's why it's not working on me."

"Why not?"

"I'm not a woman." I felt silly and serious at the same time.

"You're more like a girl." He caught on quickly.

"That's it. I'm a nature girl." A breeze fanned at us, which I found reassuring.

"Listen, my back-to-nature nymph. Would you like to come with me or wait here while I get a drink? I need to get back to my unnatural activities."

"I'll come along as long as we come right back out here. Look, you can even see some stars tonight."

He offered me his hand and pulled me up.

"The last time I saw stars, I had fallen down and hit my head. They were real beauties, almost as brilliant as you, my dear."

As I followed him into the Gandy Dancer Saloon, I felt happy with this man, and with this moment in time when I didn't know where the evening would take us.

Chapter 14

"I thank you for coming on short notice, especially since we just met on Monday with Carol. I don't know how to tell you this, but I think we should all be prepared before this hits the media."

Isis sat in our circle of thirteen looking somber in black pants and shirt. We'd all come to her house again for a special meeting she'd called at the last minute. She wore no makeup and looked tired tonight, with redness around her eyes as if she'd been crying.

"What is it, Isis?" Maria asked, sitting beside her. "What's wrong?"

"Flo Pohaski, who participated with us in the rituals for several years, has been found dead."

For a few stunned, silent seconds we looked at each other in disbelief, hoping Isis was wrong.

"But how did you find out?" I asked her. "I don't think it's even been on the news yet."

"It will be soon. Bad news always travels fast, especially news as bad as this." She shivered and tried to smile.

"To answer your question, Moonbeam, I've been in contact with police where Flo lived. I stumbled into the information today shortly after they received it from elsewhere. Flo's remains were found up north. Actually, they found the spot a few days ago, but kept it quiet until she was identified."

"Who would want to kill Flo?" Diana asked.

"Perhaps it had something to do with the group she joined. Remember she wrote us to tell us about her powerful new group?" Maria said.

"That must be it. We knew she was in danger, but didn't know where she was. Flo could be a very foolish person. Did the police have ideas about her death?" I said, looking at Isis.

"It's not natural causes. That was ruled out entirely. Unless you think being burned at the stake is a natural event."

"What!" the twelve of us said nearly as one.

"She was found in the forest by Eagle Scouts who were on a hiking trip. They were in a remote part of the woods and came upon a small clearing. The snow had drifted, revealing the charred remains of a fire. They figured it was a substantial blaze because a few nearby trees were blackened and damaged.

"Being Eagle Scouts, they examined the remains of the burning. They found bones, including an intact skull. A piece of wood in the ground, as well as wood fragments, suggested the cross.

"All in all, I never imagined we'd come up with such an ending for Flo. The facts are far darker than I ever expected. I don't know what to make of it." Isis stared at the candles burning in our circle's center. I remembered how her tarot reading weeks ago had predicted disaster, now confirmed.

"This may sound gruesome, but how did they identify her?" I asked.

"Good question. They found Flo's car stashed in a remote area several weeks before, so the remains were checked with her dental records. If her car hadn't been found she may have never been identified. It's all in the timing," Isis said.

We talked quietly together for a long time until Maria spoke up.

"How about a ritual to gather strength for the coming days? Our intent could be healing for anyone connected with Flo, for us, and for her spirit which has entered the unseen world. Do you think that we should try something like that?"

Some nodded heads, others were vocal, but we were all in agreement that performing a ritual would be beneficial. Isis dug out some old routine we'd done before, pulling papers from a desk in the ritual room where we sat and fixed the altar.

The words felt wooden as we read and moved together, but I felt real comfort and saw it in the eyes of others. As we proceeded, the room warmed up and the candles on the altar looked brighter. No electric lights spoiled the magic.

We sang familiar songs, held hands, and circled the altar with its steadily burning tapers. We stopped and spoke of Flo, directing energy to her, wherever she was.

Then Isis spoke of Flo, being real about her, about how her negativity affected our circle. I could hear her voice grow husky as she spoke of their final conversation, when Isis and then Kate had asked Flo to look at her behavior and how it affected our entire group.

"I ask the Goddess to forgive me if I played any part in Flo's death. I was just being honest, trying to do what was best for the group." I could see tears trailing down Isis's face.

"It wasn't your fault. You didn't do anything wrong," Jennifer said, who was roundish and even more childlike than the rest of us.

"Besides, there's more to this than we see. We're just understanding this on a superficial level. There's lots more beneath the surface. Whoever Flo turned to—they weren't nice people," Judy said.

Isis dried her face on her shirt sleeve and sniffled, then recovered herself sufficiently to announce, "Let's sing the last song."

She led us, and we held hands, lifting them high till the last note, when the room went completely dark.

Murmurs of alarm broke out around the circle, and I could hear Maria say, "Don't worry, I'll light the candles as soon as I grope for the matches."

I stepped back, feeling the wall behind me until I found the switch and turned the overhead light on. We blinked and smiled, and I felt shivers up my back ending in one big upper body shake.

"It looked like someone blew the candles out. Is that what everybody else saw?" Isis said.

"That's what I saw," I said, and everyone else agreed. "Did any of you blow the candles out?" Isis asked, and we all denied it.

"I don't even know if it could be engineered from where we were standing. We were too far away," Maria said.

"No windows open. The door was closed—no drafts," Judy said.

"I think it was Flo. She was communicating with us," Isis said.

Another silence, but the women soon gathered up their belongings and said good night. There was little socializing that night following Circle. We were all dealing with this trauma in whatever way we best could.

"I'll stay if you want," I said to Isis as we picked up papers and straightened the ritual room.

"Stay?" she said, still looking very distraught.

"Stay a few hours, at least until the news is over. Moral support."

"I need that, Moonbeam. I need all the moral support I can get." She hugged me tightly, and I knew my decision was sound.

We walked into the vestibule connecting the downstairs rooms before the grand sweeping staircase that led to the upper two floors.

"The television is upstairs. I don't keep one down here. This is the magical floor." Isis flashed me a smile. "Burt is probably upstairs, too."

I glanced at my watch—nearly ten o'clock.

"Channel 53 has news at ten. Maybe we can catch that," I said.

She nodded and we ascended, our feet falling heavily on the carpeted stairs. When we reached the top, I could hear mechanical noises, like the printout of a computer.

"He's in here." Isis pointed to a side room. At a modern computer desk, the only piece of non-antique furniture I'd seen in the house, sat a small, thin man with a full white beard and a bountiful head of white hair.

He turned, obviously immersed in his project, and waved and smiled.

"This is Stephanie," Isis said from the door. "She stayed after Circle. Moral support."

"Hello, Stephanie. I'm pleased to meet you. I'll be providing supportive care after I get this chapter done, Deborah. I'm pleased Stephanie has come over to join us."

We nodded, turned, and stopped in the hall.

"I was lucky to find Burt. I knew I wanted an older man who would take care of me."

She led me right into their bedroom, which was dominated by a four-poster bed with dark, carved wood. A mauve bedspread was decorated with gold suns and moons and pink, sheer chiffon curtains hung all around.

Across from the bed's foot an old dark chest of drawers supported the only television set I'd seen in this house of yesteryear. The set was small; I was almost surprised when Isis pressed the remote control and the screen burst into color.

I'd expected black-and-white.

"Have a seat," Isis said, motioning to the bed. We flopped onto the comforter, on our stomachs facing the small screen. Isis produced fluffy gold pillows to support us.

"In just a few minutes our news at ten o'clock," announced the picture-perfect woman news anchor. "Stay tuned for these stories: weapons found in a local elementary school, more flooding along our rivers, and a bizarre story about a local woman found dead—burned at the stake."

We both swallowed hard when we finally heard it broadcast. It sounded a lot worse coming across the television set—more real, more final.

"I'm glad you found out about this ahead of time, Isis. It would have been a worse shock getting the news from TV."

"I'm not sure you always get the most accurate story from the media, anyway," Isis said, her eyes glued to the screen. "I think we'll be able to piece together more information than they get."

"We have a greater interest and are personally involved," I said.

"That's what I mean. I'm not going to settle for second-hand information. Look!" she said, pointing to the screen.

I settled down upon the pillow as a female newscaster began talking of the "woman of the woods," as if Flo had been some forest dweller.

We both became deathly quiet, sitting up on our elbows, instantly alert. We knew if Flo were still alive she'd be mighty proud.

Flo had hit the big time.

Chapter 15

"This woman has been identified as Flo Pohaski, a former social worker from Pittsburgh," the reporter said, which gave the entire episode finality. Somehow I had hoped it was all a mistake.

The reporter interviewed the Eagle Scouts, whose eager fresh faces leant it all credibility. They looked honest and trustworthy as they recounted the scene they'd stumbled upon.

"So the charred remnants suggest that this woman may have been burned at the stake," the pretty, blonde reporter said, and all three scouts nodded solemnly.

I expected it to be over, but someone had been doing homework. There were two more interviews; Flo was getting attention beyond her wildest expectations.

The first was with a fellow social worker who worked where Flo had. His name was Robert, and he said he'd known Flo.

"But not well. I don't think anyone knew her well. She was into some weird religion, and she didn't have much time for any of us. She was strange."

Isis and I began to giggle, but stifled ourselves as the last interview began. A neighbor was interviewed next, and we looked at each other with raised eyebrows, for Flo had no close neighbors. Evidently Flo had talked to this woman somewhere along the line.

“I’m shocked. She seemed like a nice enough person. I only talked to her a few times, but she was some sort of witch. She was real proud of it, too. She was a witch and she got burned at the stake. Sort of odd, don’t you think?” said the woman dressed in casual clothes, claiming to be a neighbor.

“And so, this mystery is far from being solved—a loner who claimed to be a witch who was burned at the stake in remote forest land. This is Cynthia Hartsock for Channel 53 news.”

I felt depressed now, after the official news investigation.

“That gives witches a really great image,” Isis said.

“We go off into the woods and self-destruct in a puff of smoke,” I added. “I wonder what really happened.”

Isis sat with her chin in her hands, lying on her stomach on the bed.

“I’m not one to wonder, Moonbeam. I intend to find out the truth. I won’t rest until I find out what happened to Flo.”

“How will you do that?” I felt puzzled and uneasy at the same time.

“We,” she said, staring pointedly at me. “We will find out.” She poked me in the ribs with one finger.

"Just for the sake of this conversation I agree to 'we.' So how do we do that?" I dreaded her answer.

"What do you think?"

"We meditate and wait for the answer to appear out of the haze?"

"Very funny. Not a bad second line of offense. No, the plan of action will be more direct than that."

"Tell me."

"We go up there and do our own investigating. We study the site where she died and try to find out about the group she joined. We should be able to locate them," she said proudly.

"Now, Isis," I said firmly, "chances are Flo didn't crawl up on that cross and burn herself."

Isis looked stumped. "What do you mean?"

"This is murder. Someone killed her. This is a job for professionals."

"I'm not afraid to take it on."

"Well, I am. If someone burned her, they could just as easily do away with any witches asking about her. Nosing around could be more than dangerous. It could be fatal. And fatal is forever."

She looked as if she considered my words. When she spoke up again, her enthusiasm was considerably dampened.

"I can go myself. You don't have to go with me. I'll understand." Her words were quiet and thoughtful.

I heaved a big sigh. "Let me think about it. I'm not sure it feels safe to me."

"I'll have to go soon. I want to start investigating right away, before the place is overrun with national news reporters."

"How long will you be gone?" I asked.

"I'm not sure yet. At least overnight. It's about a three hour drive to get up there. I guess it would depend on what I find."

"One overnight would be all I could manage with my work schedule. And Tricksie doesn't like me to go away. I'll let you know as soon as I can, and if you've already left, I'll understand.

"But Isis, I know where you propose to go is a dark and dangerous place."

* * *

I awoke the next morning feeling fresh and hopeful. Tricksie had stationed herself down by my feet, and she rumbled out loud, volleys of purring. I held still to see if it shook the bed, but by some mystical law of physics, it didn't.

I smoothed her incredibly soft fur and thought of nothing else for the moment. I briefly wondered about Hank and his whereabouts, and when he might turn up next. I realized I missed him more than a little.

"Maybe that's a good sign, Tricks," I told her, and she looked up at me as if she understood. "Maybe I'll be able to have a relationship."

My tongue twisted slightly when I said the "r" word, so that it came out distorted. Trickster understood, anyway.

The universe exhibits a strange sense of humor at times, and this was one of those times. The phone rang insistently till I answered it, and I had a strong feeling it might actually be Hank.

"Hello," I said in my most sultry voice.

"Well, don't we sound sexy today? Maybe I ought to come right over," the man said. I could picture him standing there talking into his cell phone.

"Alex?"

"At least you haven't completely forgotten me. I thought our evening together was memorable."

"How did you get my number? I don't remember giving you the home phone number."

"I'd like to claim to be some sort of wizard with special powers, but you did tell me your last name, Ms. Gray. Are you aware your number is in the phone book?"

I snorted and felt foolish.

"Listen, lady, that last date was pretty short. I'd like to continue it this evening or at your earliest convenience. What do you say?"

I swallowed and did some fast thinking.

"A friend of mine has invited me on a short trip. I'm not even sure if I can go along, but I need to decide about that first. Can I get back to you later about this?"

"I hope he's not as good-looking and congenial as I am."

"She. It's a girlfriend. She wants me to go with her, but I haven't made up my mind yet."

"You have my cell phone number, don't you?"

"Yes."

"Call me when you know something. I'll leave this evening free in case you're available."

"No need to do that. Go ahead and make your plans," I said, hoping he would.

I thought I heard him laughing, then the connection ended.

Yes, I'd enjoyed our evening together at Station Square, when time had rolled by like the flow of the Mon River.

But I didn't miss Alex, hadn't given him much thought since that night.

It was Hank I missed.

Chapter 16

When I flipped the television set on a few minutes later and saw it on the news again—Flo, the woman of the woods—I suddenly knew.

I knew I had to go with Isis.

She wouldn't be safe without me, and together we could make some sense of this muddle. Then again, I wasn't convinced this was any of our business after all. Flo had disinherited us before she died. What did her death have to do with us?

First, I checked the weather for the next two days—only possible snow flurries predicted. No problem with traveling. I sighed and picked up the cordless phone, the decision made despite my inner protestations. Isis answered, and we made quick plans to meet in an hour.

"We'll travel light," Isis said. "Just throw your toothbrush in your purse."

"I have to be back tomorrow by three, Deborah. Luckily, I'm off today," I said.

After a thoughtful silence, she said, "That should work. We'll just have to make it work. And if one trip doesn't get us enough information, we'll go back until we're done."

After we rang off, I punched in Alex's cell phone number. It barely rang before he answered.

"Alex, I hope I'm not interrupting anything."

"Ah, that's the beauty of these little beauties. I'm walking Tommy—nothing too pornographic at the present moment. This is Stephanie, I hope?"

"Yes. Do you have a son?"

"He's grown. You mean Tommy? He's a boxer and my favorite buddy. Of course, I like you better. Are we getting together later on tonight?"

"That's why I called. I'm going along with Deborah, and we'll be gone overnight. I'll get back in time for work tomorrow. I'd love to see you again. Maybe later on in the week?"

"I love to grovel and supplicate myself as far as women go. No problem. I'll get back to you later in the week. By the way, where is it that you're going?"

I coughed to buy myself a few seconds and divert his attention. My inner bell was ding-donging loudly, alerting me to a no-go situation. I knew I should tell him as little as possible.

"My friend has a sick relative and wants to go right away before it's too late." Flo was very sick indeed, and our Circle sister. I hated to tell an outright lie.

"But where?"

"She hasn't told me exactly yet. It could be somewhere in Ohio." Or maybe in Alaska or Texas, I thought, holding my breath.

"You be careful. I'll have to drown my misery in wild revelry tonight. Somehow, I'll survive. Tell Aunt Hattie or whoever it is to get better fast."

The line clicked, and I almost forgot I needed to throw a few things together for the trip. I was still immersed in the conversation with Alex.

He affected me that way.

I tossed stuff into a red athletic bag, almost forgetting toiletries and underwear. I knew I'd forget something. I always did.

Tricksie seemed to realize something was up. While I stepped into the bathroom to gather my toothbrush and paste, I heard her cry. I could just see the tips of her ears when I reentered the bedroom.

"I'd like to take you along, Miss Kitty," I said, staring into my open bag where she'd packed herself. She looked up at me and purred loudly.

"You don't like to travel, though, Tricksie. You cry the whole time." I hauled her off my smashed clothes in the bag and rocked her.

"I'll be back tomorrow. You'll be fine. I put out extra food and water." I eyed her plump figure and juggled her considerable weight, then put her down on the bed.

"Now don't eat all of your food for tomorrow today," I said, stroking her ears.

Tricksie lay on her back as I zipped the bag, and I kissed her fur head.

"Mah," she said, and I let her have the last word. That always worked best for us.

* * *

We met at King's Restaurant, a halfway point on our destination. Isis was already there in her red Dodge. She pulled out, motioning me to park in her space.

"I'll drive," she said. "This is my hare-brained scheme. Hop in."

My red bag and I barely hit the interior of the car before we were under way. We had not a minute to lose, or so it felt.

"Isis, you're driving like this is an emergency. Is this an emergency?" I asked as she drove through a light turned red for several of my accelerated heartbeats.

"Oh, dear. Am I being reckless? I do have this sense of urgency, Moonbeam."

"I agree that we need to be timely, and we are. We're making this trip right away to investigate Flo's murder. But we must stay centered and stay in the moment. We'll learn more that way. Rushing will only make us lose track of the signs. Please forgive me for preaching."

She smiled, breathing deeply.

"As always, you ground me. My energies tend to be scattered, poorly focused. That's one reason why I wanted you to come along."

We rode along in silence for a few minutes.

"By the way, Moonbeam, where are we going?"

I examined the road map, searching for the little town up north where the newscast had originated about Flo. I finally found it—a small dot where there were few small dots. These were the outer reaches of civilization. I as a city girl could hardly imagine living so far from the crowds.

"We just stay on 28 north until we hit Kittanning, then we go on smaller roads until we find this place. It's called Apple Grove, and it must be a secluded grove of a town after all, because it's located on an unpaved road," I said.

"There are towns on unpaved roads? With my spiritual beliefs, I lean toward back-to- nature and the power of creation, but an unpaved road?"

Isis was a city girl, too. Here we were, headed for the forest and the realm of the Goddess, knowing only our city ways.

"Looks like we have a few things to learn. It's in the Allegheny National Forest. There's lots of forest land here. I'd say we're going to be out of our element," I said, still searching the map.

"We were both witches before, and I'm sure over the centuries we've come from forest communities. Some of them probably didn't have roads of any kind. We'll just make the best of this. I think I'm going to be glad you came along with me, Stephanie."

We talked and rode, and the miles passed. Our four-lane road would soon give way to two-lane roads. Our pace was steady, yet not rushed. When we had left the city behind, I marveled at the rolling hills and wooded areas. It always came as a surprise to me, this view of rural America—Pennsylvania, more specifically.

"It's so beautiful out here," I spoke in true awe. "I always forget what it's like out here, outside the city. It's as if I'm so submerged in city life I forget what else there is."

Isis looked over at me. "City witches leaving the city—on holiday to rediscover our roots, maybe."

"I wish we had another reason for coming out here other than Flo. But for her, we wouldn't be in this beautiful place. Funny how things are turning out."

"Let's just pretend it's the full moon, too, which would intensify all our efforts. Maybe that will give us an extra edge on finding information."

I smiled. "I'm very good at make believe. It helps."

We had come to Clarion at the end of the four-lane, and I had little idea what lay beyond. We stopped at a Wendy's and were able to scrape together a vegetarian lunch. In the land of the two-lane roads, we weren't sure if we'd easily find food.

"This might be our last decent meal until tomorrow," Isis said.

"We'll find something. I hope we can find a place for the night. We might need a tent or something equally primitive."

"All those news people made it up here, and they survived, so we'll do just fine. And I did throw a tent in for a true emergency."

"You go camping, Isis?" I asked in amazement.

"To tell you the truth, I haven't opened the tent since 1989."

Chapter 17

"This road never ends. I drive and drive and drive and we never go anywhere. See that pine tree over there. I could swear we already passed it before," Isis said. The dust flew around her little car as we crunched along on the gravel road to somewhere, I still hoped and believed.

"We're getting there. And these pine trees disguise themselves to trick the tourists. Just a little forest humor. But we're just creeping on this joke-for-a-road. We don't have roads like this in the city."

By my minute-by-minute scrutiny of the map, we had to be getting close to Apple Grove. We'd driven about four hours, including our lunch stop, so it was late afternoon by now. Both of us were anxious to get there.

"What's that up ahead?" I asked. In the distance, there appeared to be buildings.

"It's a mirage. We've been on this damned road so long that we're now hallucinating. This gravel and dirt stretches forever—from tree to shining tree."

As we drew near, I felt a sense of relief that we were actually arriving. I knew it was the right place; there were news trucks parked everywhere. In fact, the news trucks outnumbered the buildings by two to one.

A tiny sign read "Apple Grove." I applauded loudly, and Isis hooted her heartiest. She pulled off beside the road and we stared at what there was of Apple Grove.

There didn't appear to be much to it.

"You can't expect anything too big off an unpaved road," I told Isis, who shook her head in disbelief.

This patch of buildings had evidently sprung up to service hunters and campers in the forest. The grocery store stood small and rundown-looking. A service station with one pump and a white wooden exterior also served as the U.S. Post Office. Three small log houses and a trailer looked to be the residential district, and wonder of wonders—I saw a silver diner and a small motel.

"It has everything we need. This place is perfect," Isis said, and I looked at her closely to see if she was being sarcastic. No, she really meant it.

She pulled in at the motel, and we entered the office with high hopes for the night.

"Could we get a room for the night?" Isis asked an old man who looked as if we'd interrupted his sleep.

"Let me see. I think all the rooms have been taken by the news people." He shuffled papers, cleared his throat, and looked at us through thick lenses with black plastic frames. His eyes, faded blue and rheumy, were nearly obscured by the lenses.

A key lay on the desk, the yellow plastic tag reading "103." I wondered if someone had checked out and left it there.

"What about this room? Did someone just check out?" Isis sounded a little frantic. I was holding my breath, as I wasn't too keen on spending the night like brownie scouts in Isis's tent.

The white-haired man stared at the key, picked it up, and turned it over absent-mindedly. His hands were knotted and shook slightly as he rattled the key.

"Oh, yes, one young gentleman got another assignment and had to leave today. He thought someone would be coming up from the station to replace him. He wanted me to save the room for the next guy."

"We'll take the room," Isis said, getting her wallet out of a brown, leather-fringed purse.

"I suppose I ought to save this room for the newsperson," the man said, turning the key over in his hand.

"What if he doesn't come until tomorrow? We just need the room this one night," I said, wanting to say instead, "We'll freeze to death in a small tent during the night if you don't help us out."

He hung the key up on a board that was empty.

"We're news people, too. We're reporters for the newspaper. We need to get information for an article," Isis said, and I successfully suppressed a smile.

The man looked up and looked interested. Or maybe he had gas pains.

"Women's Circle News. It's a small, but intellectual publication based out of Pittsburgh. Here's my press card." Isis flashed a card from her wallet at the man.

He looked up with greater respect in his face.

"Room 103." He held out the key. "Sorry I haven't much to offer you. Maybe I should check the room and see if it's been cleaned."

"No problem, sir. The room will be just fine. We'll stop back if anything needs done," I said quickly, grabbing the key as Isis filled out the paperwork and paid.

We jumped in the red car and drove a short distance and pulled before room 103,

"Isis, what press card?" I asked.

"It was my library card. It looks pretty official, and I get desperate when there's a tent involved."

Once inside the room with our small bags, Isis and I let loose all the suppressed laughter until I felt weak and my stomach hurt.

"Some news guy is going to be very mad at us. But I'll be a good sport about it," Isis said.

"You mean you'll give up the room?"

"Better than that," she said, a crazed gleam in her eye.

"You'll ask him to join us?" I believed in being ridiculous.

"No, I'll give him the tent."

Minutes later, we'd put away our sparse belongings. The musty smell had hit me as I'd first walked into the small room with its double bed and faded, dated look. The bedspread, a pastel floral print, was all that brightened the décor in here, and it must have been washed a hundred times.

I could hear the sound of water running in the toilet tank—running and running and running. A plastic floral arrangement that must have dated back to the sixties graced a battered chest of drawers. The flowers looked ultra-tacky against the dark brown fake wood panel walls.

"The room is perfect," Isis said.

"I agree. Maybe we can come back later for a month of vacation."

"I was serious." She even looked solemn, not her natural state.

"I know, I know. For Apple Grove, these are plush accommodations. I'm not trying to be ungrateful; I guess I'm focused on our search." I had my fingers crossed behind me. Shall we get started?"

"Yes, Moonbeam. By the way, one last question, my friend."

"Yes?"

"Where are we going now?"

* * *

Every group needs a plan of action, a brilliant overview of the big picture. We would have liked to have rested a while from our trip, soaked up the atmosphere in our room, but there was no time for that. We were forced to push onward in our search for clues.

"I know where we go next." My inspiration felt brilliant.

"Yeah?"

"I say we go to the diner."

"Why the diner?"

"The diner is the center of a community of people, especially those who are out and about, in the know. You'd be surprised what you can find out in a diner. It's a hub for salt-of-the-earth people. I think if we start there we'll get a good lead," I said with more confidence than I really felt.

"You should know about diners. Let's head over there. We sure aren't going to learn much from the guy who runs this motel," Isis said.

We crunched over there in our sneakers, the gravel grounding us with the sound and uncertain footing. The sun was shining, making the town look hospitable and making us feel warm in our winter coats. It had been thirty degrees at home, probably colder here up north. We passed the service station/post office, and the garage man nodded at us. I idly wondered if he cleaned the grease off his hands before he sorted the mail.

The diner was small, neat, and silver, with its large parking lot, and I felt my first stirrings of hope as we neared its doors.

I imagined the locals ate early, and the place was fairly inhabited now at four o'clock. I eyed the counter and large dining room. Several tables held crews of news people—too urban-looking for this part of the state.

A waitress led us to a table in the far corner of the dining room, and we sat down.

"Maybe we ought to sit closer to the middle," Isis said, not even looking at the menu.

"This is my favorite spot. We can see everyone in the diner. We won't miss a thing," I said.

"But who do we ask what?" Isis chewed on a fingernail.

"Let's order some food. After all, we've got to eat. By the time we're done, we'll have some answers."

"We just ate a couple of hours ago," Isis said after consulting her watch.

"You hungry?"

"Believe it or not, I am."

"So we'll eat early, then we'll be hot on Flo's trail in just minutes. I hate to take this time out to eat, but this investment in time will pay off big."

The waitress returned, a chunky girl who looked untidy. Her short brunette hair stuck out at odd angles, her plaid shirt tail partially pulled out of her jeans.

"You ladies ready to order?" Her voice had a drawl to it, but was still pleasant to the ear.

"Sure. We're in a bit of a hurry. You see, we just got here and we have to report on the Flo Pohaski story for our magazine. We only have till tomorrow morning."

"You and every other person who has walked into this diner the past few days. I mean the Flo Pohaski thing. I can't imagine what the fuss is over some poor old woman who died up here."

"Do you know how we can find the place where she was burned? Our editor expects us to get pictures," I said. Isis's eyes were burning holes in her menu.

"I tell you what. You two give me your order, and I'll put it in, then I'll talk to you. Or else you won't have time to make your search." She stood poised with pad at our command. I read her name tag.

"Thank you, Kim," I said, knowing I could trust this fellow waitress, a bond as strong as sister.

Isis ordered the chef salad with cheese only, no meat, and I ordered tuna salad and potato soup. We sat back and waited with rising expectations.

Chapter 18

Kim returned in only a few minutes without her ordering pad, looking rushed.

"Can you sit down for a minute?" Isis said, moving the empty chair beside her.

"Thanks, I'll stand. Boss might be looking. Customers might be paying attention. You said you want to see where Flo Pohaski was killed."

"Yes. We actually knew her. So we have a strong reason for getting the story," I said.

"Where she was killed was up in the woods, far back. Honestly, I don't think you would have time tonight to go there and investigate. It'll be dark soon. Someone can take you in the morning. You'll have better luck that way," Kim said, glancing over her shoulder.

"Do you know someone who can take us?" Isis asked.

"Sure, I'll find someone. Are you staying at the motel?" We nodded. I gave Kim our room number and she promised to call us first thing in the morning.

"What if she doesn't call us?" Isis asked after the waitress left.

"We'll find someone to direct us to the spot. We just have to get up bright and early."

"And what are we doing tonight, then?"

I wondered at her childlike trust of me. With her capabilities, she could have easily handled these situations if I hadn't come along.

"We still need to find out about the group she belonged to. That's probably more important than seeing where she died. We need to ask questions, Isis."

Kim came back with our food, and we ate it thoughtfully. It tasted great—simple, yet nourishing. Only part of my mind lingered on the food, though. Our time here was so limited that I began to wonder if I should have taken tomorrow off work.

We finished quickly, saying goodbye to Kim before we left. I honestly thought she'd come through with her offer of help. A good waitress means what she says.

I gazed at the tables of diners, wanting to speak with the locals and even the news crews. But interrupting someone's meal was against the rules.

We'd find out somehow.

When we'd gotten outside, Isis stretched and smiled. "Where to, Moonbeam?"

"Let's go for a little walk up the road."

Forest surrounded us, except for these few buildings and vehicles. I noticed how clean the air smelled and almost forgot our mission in my enjoyment of the natural environment. It didn't look like a place

Flo would have frequented. Despite her connections as a witch, she seemed mostly a city girl.

A creek bubbled down a hill and across a yard near where we walked. Outside a weathered trailer, an older woman stood.

"Here I go," I muttered to Isis. I walked into the yard, feeling conscious I was trespassing on this lady's land. "Excuse me, ma'am, but I was wondering if I could ask you a few questions."

"I suppose you can. I don't have many answers, though." She wore a black fleece jacket, and her green cotton house dress fluttered around her, accentuating her slender figure that belied her white hair.

"We just came to Apple Grove today to find out about our friend Flo Pohaski. Have you heard about her?" I asked.

"My, yes, everyone's heard about her. You'd think she was born and raised here, but she wasn't. She was an outsider, not native to these parts."

"Do you know why she came here?"

"I don't think she came here to get burned up crispy like that. I don't think anyone can figure out what she was up to."

I glanced at Isis before continuing. "Flo told us she was involved with some group up here. Did you hear anything about that?"

She scratched her head without mussing her white coiffure. "You know, I never met this woman. I don't think any of us ever saw her when she was alive. She never came to Apple Grove to my knowledge."

Oh, you would have remembered Flo. By the way Isis was grinning, she must have had the same happy thought.

"And the group?" I gently reminded the lady.

"Lands, yes, I forgot about that. No groups here. I never heard mention of any, either. Those Eagle Scouts were the closest to a group I can think of. Is that what you mean?" Her gentle blue eyes made her look young and girlish.

"I don't think the Eagle Scouts would have wanted her."

"If you look around you, you'll see we don't have groups here. Not enough people. Little clumps are about the best we can do." The woman seemed to be enjoying our conversation; she'd become animated and showed no signs of hurry. I appreciated her help, but I wasn't getting any information.

"We thank you for your time. You've been very helpful. We'll be going on now," I said and started to turn back to the road.

"Can I get you something to drink?"

"We just ate at the diner, but thank you, anyway. Thanks again for your help."

She sat down in a green plastic chair in her yard, looking lost, as we moved on down the road. I figured she didn't get much company.

"What next?" Isis asked, and she sounded amused.

Before I could answer, we'd come to the combination garage and post office. I could see the mechanic working under the hood of a battered blue pick-up truck. I approached this one with more hesitation, as he appeared to be busy.

"You want to take this one?" I asked Isis.

"I suppose I could. After all, I'd be doing all this myself if you hadn't come along, Moonbeam."

She took a deep breath before continuing.

"Sir," she said hopefully, "could I have a word with you?"

He pulled his head from under the hood, scowling, but when he saw Isis, he smiled and pulled off his blue ball cap. Long brown hair streaked with gray fell down and covered part of his tanned face accentuated by manly wrinkles.

Isis stood there in rust coat with fake fur trimmings, her tie-dyed jumper, and burnt orange turtleneck and I realized what we had here—two old hippies.

"I'm not a sir, ma'am," he said. "I'm a Ralph. And who are you two ladies?" He was looking straight at Isis, like he'd just been born a gosling and he'd imprinted on her.

"I'm Deborah, and this is my friend Stephanie."

"How can I help you two ladies? Did your car break down?"

"No, Ralph, nothing like that. We're just looking for information. We were friends of Flo Pohaski. Did you know her at all?"

He tossed his head, and the long hair flipped gracefully in the air.

"I don't think she ever came to Apple Grove. If she did, nobody noticed her. It's been business as usual for years here. This is the first excitement since that big black bear tried to break into Joe McKinncy's hunting cabin, and that was five years ago."

Isis fluttered her eyelashes. I almost laughed out loud, for Ralph was definitely under her power. And it was genuine—we witches don't do spells in such matters—her earth mother magnetism drew him.

"Flo wrote us and said she belonged to a group. Anything like that around here? Do you know of any groups or even cults in this area?"

He stared at the truck engine with great intensity. "No groups up here I know of. This is a small place, as you can see, but there's a lot of forest here. It can get pretty wild and primitive. And there are private residences and hunting camps. What goes on there would be confidential, so long as no rules are broken or no one finds out. This isn't suburbia."

Isis smiled. "You've been very helpful, Ralph. Please forgive us for interrupting your work."

"You can interrupt me any time, Ms. Deborah. This has been a real pleasure. We don't get many lovely city ladies such as yourselves in this hamlet."

She turned red, and I marveled that Ralph could make her blush.

"Thank you," she said.

"Now if you want to hang out at some point during your visit, I'd love to be your guide to Apple Grove."

"Ralph, how kind of you. Stephanie and I have only a few hours here. We'll be leaving in the morning."

"I'll be here tinkering if you change your mind. If you come back some other time, please come and see me." He sounded real, solid, and totally enchanted with Isis.

Isis handed Ralph her business card with phone number, then we waved goodbye as we walked back to the street. I took her elbow and steered her in the direction we'd come from.

"Femme fatale," I murmured with a devilish smile.

"We hippies gravitate toward each other. It's a peace, love, let's-get-naked thing." She spoke at a discreet volume.

When we'd proceeded beyond hearing range, we both cut loose and roared again, the belly laughter rejuvenating us. We gasped together like high school girlfriends, our mission temporarily forgotten.

"It's good to know that there's a new life waiting for me somewhere. When I'm having a bad day, that will comfort me," Isis said, who was Deborah in Apple Grove.

We were headed back for the motel, retracing our tracks, not particularly paying attention to our pathway. I looked as we passed the trailer, but the woman who had spoken to us had vanished.

"What about those people there? Maybe they could help us," Isis said, pointing to two men walking toward a news truck. They had just come out of the diner.

"Guess we'd better try." I felt in awe of the professionals. My anxiety level shot up. "You want to handle this one?"

"Your turn?"

We were nearly upon them, and one man had his hand on the door handle of the truck. “Excuse me, we were wanting to ask you gentlemen a couple of questions. You’re here from Channel 11 News?” I asked, reading off the truck’s side.

“Yes, I’m Rich Fillmore, cameraman and truck driver. This is my buddy Tom Waits—he’s the reporter. I say it with pictures, he says it with words. But who are you? You don’t look like locals.” The man was big and good-natured looking, with dark hair and beard. With his jean jacket, blue plaid shirt and jeans, he fit right in with the natives.

“We drove up from Pittsburgh today and we’ve never been here before. I’m Stephanie and this is my friend Deborah. We wanted to investigate what happened to Flo Pohaski because she was a friend of ours.”

“You knew Flo Pohaski?” Tom asked. I noticed the reporter’s thinning light brown hair, silver-rimmed glasses, and slender build. His camel wool jacket, blue shirt, and dress pants separated him from the residents of this place—a blatant fashion mistake.

“Yes, we weren’t good friends, but she belonged to our women’s group. When she disappeared, we worried about her,” Isis said.

“Looks like the news is coming to us today,” Tom said, slapping Rich’s broad back. “You can’t believe how little information we’ve been able to uncover on this woman. It’s as if she lived in a vacuum.

“Ladies, can we interview you for Channel 11 News?”

Chapter 19

"Actually, we were hoping to ask you a few questions, Tom. We've come a long way and we want to find out what happened to our friend," I said, knowing I didn't want to be interviewed.

"Shall we step back into the diner and sit and talk?" Rich asked.

Isis looked at me and shook her head.

"We were just in there. We've started back to the motel. You guys staying there?" Isis said. The news men nodded and agreed to meet us in their motel room in ten minutes. They were conveniently located in room 104.

After a brief stop in our luxurious room, I knocked next door and we were ushered in. The news men may have thought us bearers of hot news, but we just wanted to know what they knew.

Period.

"Have a seat on the bed there, ladies. Make yourselves comfortable," Rich said.

I nearly tripped over wadded up clothes on the floor, but both beds had been neatly made up (maybe by the old man who had checked us in). We settled on the bed and tried not to focus on the beer cans on the bedside stand.

"So, Stephanie, can you tell me about the group you and Flo belonged to?" Tom asked, seated beside Rich on the other double bed. Rich had turned on the television and was watching intently with the sound low.

"I'd like you to answer our questions first, Tom. Have you any idea what happened to Flo?" I said.

"If you've been listening to the news, you know as much as I do. Some scouts found the spot up in the woods. She was identified from dental records. We can't find anyone who knew her or remembers her being up here. It's as if aliens dropped her here."

"I could buy that one," Isis said.

"Me, too," I said. "Have you run into any group that she belonged to? She wrote us a note and said she'd joined another group."

"Like I said, ladies, we have almost nothing, and we're just about to pull out of Apple Grove and drive back to the city. I did ask locals and the law enforcement here if she had any connection with anyone here, and I drew a blank. So, ladies, it's my turn. Can you fill in the blanks for me?"

We answered his questions as best we could, firmly stating we did not wish our names to be used, and certainly did not want to be videotaped.

"Why all this secrecy? You seem like very genuine, up-front type people," Tom said.

"Please keep in mind that our friend Flo was brutally murdered and belonged to our group," Isis said.

"There may be no connection, but we're witches, too, and we don't want her murderers on our trail," I said.

"People have funny ideas about witches, based on mythology, half-truths, and black witchcraft. If you put us on television, you can bet we'll get threatening phone calls and all sorts of negative attention. No, thank you, gentlemen," Isis said.

"Let me get your last names for my record. How is yours spelled, Stephanie?" Tom sat poised with note pad and pen.

"N-o," I said.

He wrinkled his eyebrows. "Okay, I give up. It's been a pleasure to meet you two. It was an even exchange of information; we gave you very little, and you gave us about the same. Of course you know you can contact us if anything surfaces."

Tom handed me his business card with phone number and e-mail address. Rich tore himself away from his television show long enough to smile and wave goodbye. Tom held the door for us as we sauntered through.

"We'll bang on the wall if we come up with anything," Isis said.

"Make sure it's the right wall," Rich said.

Isis closed the door of their room behind us, saying in a lowered voice, "Do you think they'll try to get our names from the front desk guy?"

"Isn't that illegal or something?" I whispered back.

"It doesn't matter. I registered us under my mother's maiden name. You can't be too careful, my mother always used to say."

We quieted as we entered the sanctuary of our room. Even if we gained no insight into Flo's demise, even if we didn't find one clue, we'd at least spent a night in this prestigious establishment. Las Vegas eat your heart out.

I lost control and sputtered into laughter.

Isis looked at me sideways and smiled. "You're laughing about the room, aren't you?"

I nodded and snorted some more.

"Ah, but the tent would have made you humble and appreciative of this place. Let's see," she said and looked at her watch, "I think we have enough time to still get a camping site and set up for the night. Of course, I forgot the bug spray. I wonder if they have poisonous snakes up here."

I placed a hand over my heart, what was left of it, and said, "I hereby solemnly promise to appreciate our room 103 at the Pine Needle Motel in Apple Grove and not laugh at it or put it down in any way."

Momentarily appeased, Isis visited the bathroom and I turned on the TV set. I was amazed this place had cable and got quite a few channels. I clamped my lips together and resolved to refrain from further comments.

When Isis returned, she seemed more relaxed.

"This has been a long day, what with all the traveling to get here and trying to make contact with Flo's life up here," she said. She wore a long gray nightshirt with fairies on it. "I sometimes get the feeling we'll figure this out, but the clues won't come from here."

"Where will they come from?" As usual, Isis had me mystified.

"From the city. From Pittsburgh."

"So what are we doing up here?"

"It seemed like the logical place to start. And there will be clues here. There have to be some."

I pondered this as she changed the channel, wondering how the city could provide any clues. I tried to settle into a psychic space and access information about these city clues. Then I attempted to divine the clues we'd extract from the forest.

But intuition sometimes fails me, and this was one of those times.

* * *

Isis and I still slept soundly early the next morning when the knocking began. A gentle tapping barely roused us, and I wondered if I dreamed about elves making shoes in some forest workshop.

"Stephanie, there's someone at our door. Do we have a gun? Who knows we're here?" Isis's hair stuck out in strange ways above her half-closed eyes.

"What is it, Isis?" I was immediately awake and jumped out of bed. "I think it's forest elves. I'll let them in."

I stumbled to the door, but left the chain guard on per request of my roommate. I opened the door and peered through the crack.

"Hello, anybody out there?" I said, seeing no one.

"It's me." A small boy's face appeared in the crack. "Kim sent me to take you up to the forest to see where the woman was burned up."

"Great. Come on in."

Isis shot me an evil look, and I realized we weren't dressed. I let him in anyway.

"What's your name?" I asked him. "What time is it?"

"I'm Bo. Kim's brother. I took some news guys up there before." He stared at his watch. "6:30."

Isis had already bustled into the bathroom with her clothes.

"Bo, it's great of you to come over. Why don't you watch television while we get ready? We'll be just a few minutes getting dressed."

"Sure," he said and sat on my unmade bed with the remote control. He ran a hand through his straight brown hair and stuffed his red shirt back into his jeans. With his round face, he could have been a cherub instead of a boy nine or ten years old.

I pulled clothes from my bag, including black sweat pants and a gray and red Coca Cola T-shirt. I passed Isis as she emerged from the bathroom fully awake in the tie-dyed pants outfit. When I was dressed and ready for our journey a few minutes later, Bo seemed disappointed.

"We don't have cable," he said as he reluctantly relinquished the control.

"Now, young man, where do we go from here? Do we ride, hike, fly or canoe to get there?" I asked.

He giggled. "I like funny people," he said. "This is going to be better than taking the news guys. We ride first."

We'd managed to make it out the door of our room. A small bike sat in front of Isis's car.

"Is this what we ride? Will we all fit on it?" I asked him, pointing to the bike.

His smile was broad and sunny. "No, we have to go in your car, but not for very long. Then we get out and walk for a long time. That's why I came early." He sounded proud.

"And all those news people hiked up in the woods for a long time?" I asked.

"Not all of them. Some of them wouldn't do it. Said it wasn't that great of a news story, anyway. One guy wanted to fly in a helicopter, but there's no place close to land one. So not everyone went up there," Bo said.

Isis had completely regained her composure by now. "We're glad you got up so early to take us into the woods. We can get into the car and get started now, but first, let's put your bike in the motel room."

This day when we had awakened so abruptly from our dreams continued to have the quality of a dream. Rather than being anxious or excited to see the site of the murder, Isis and I blissfully flowed forward, unaware of the surprises ahead.

Chapter 20

"It's not much further," Bo said as we wound our way on a narrow path through the forest.

"That's what you said a half hour ago and an hour ago," Isis said. "How long does it take to get to this place?"

"I'm not exactly sure, but it takes a pretty long time. It'll go faster when we go back—it's more downhill."

We had been walking at a fast clip through dense forest for nearly an hour now. Fortunately, the snow had evidently thawed since Flo had been discovered, with little remaining, making our trek easier. I was thankful we had started so early, for I still worked that evening. Even so, at the rate we were moving, I worried about getting back in time for my shift.

"This is the tricky part. This is where we bushwhack," the boy said.

"I hope bushwhack doesn't mean what I think it means," I said.

"What's it mean?" Isis asked.

"We take off through the woods," the boy said simply.

"Isn't that what we're doing already?" Isis asked.

"We leave the trail and go on our own through the woods, making our own path. But don't worry, it's easy," Bo said.

A half hour later, I'd tripped over tree roots, been attacked by bramble bushes, and generally felt totally discouraged. I asked Bo for the tenth time, "Are you sure this is the right way to go?"

His eyes were soulful, yet not condemning. "You city people aren't much good in the woods. Hunters around these parts bushwhack all the time—for hours and sometimes days. If no one ever left the trail, your friend would have never been found."

"But when will we be there? And don't tell me it's just up the next hill." I tried not to whine.

"Soon," he said.

He gave a small yelp and started running, and it took all we had to keep up with him. That last sprint nearly finished Isis and me off. When we reached the tiny, cleared circle, he jumped up and down and pointed.

"See, I told you I could find it. It's here just like I said." He pointed to the small area roped off with yellow plastic warning banner. If it weren't for the warning signs, I wouldn't have noticed the place.

"Bo, we need to gather our thoughts about this place, so we need some privacy. Could you come back in about twenty minutes? You needn't go far. We're proud of you that you were able to find this spot," Isis said.

"No problem. I'll be back in twenty minutes. I'll just go down the hill. You can call me if you need me."

"Oh, we will," I said.

When he had gone, the energies of the place felt curious. I sat and surveyed the blackened trees nearby and the roughly circular area that had been marked off.

"What are you getting, Isis?" In matters such as these, she was often more perceptive than I was.

She stared into the circle that held charred remains of the fire. I knew instinctively that Flo's remains had been removed to some police lab. All that remained here were the impressions of that fire, of her fateful end.

"The feelings are strong. I can't blot them out," Isis said. She paced outside the circle. "She was surprised. That was the main thing she felt till the end. This thing didn't come out at all as she expected. She felt betrayed, for she had trusted someone blindly, but surprise and shock were the main emotions."

She turned to me. "What do you get, Moonbeam?"

I had already gathered my thoughts before Isis spoke. I didn't want to be influenced by her psychic impressions.

"I see some kind of diversion, something in Flo's favor, right before the end. I see her hiding something here, something of value to her that she might want to live on beyond her. She knows the end is near, yet she doesn't feel fear. At the end, she is resigned to her fate. Yes, I feel the astonishment, her disbelief or surprise, as you call it.

"There are others here, all in robes, and it's night and flames thrust up high. Flo uses her concentration and magical powers to leave her body before it is burned. She does not suffer."

I felt weak now, tired, as if I had been there, a witness to the carnage. Although fascinated by the images coming to me, a part of me wished I had never come to this place.

"Stephanie," she said gently, as if drawing me back from another time and place, "where did she hide something?"

I looked up and around, surprised myself to be here, as I'd been so immersed in the past images.

"She placed it in something. Near here, not far. She had only a few minutes to hide it. And even then she hid it before the danger became clear; she felt a foreboding and slid it away."

"There aren't many hiding places out here," Isis said. "If it's still here, she was counting on not being observed in her movements."

We searched, knowing Bo might come back at any moment, fearing his loyalties lay with the news guys. Technically, anything we found should go to the police, but Isis and I didn't exactly look at it that way.

"Here it is!" she said, extracting a bundle from a hole in a big oak not far outside the circle. I recognized a purple scarf of Flo's wrapped around the object.

Instead of opening the parcel, though, Isis stood behind me, stowing it in my backpack with a zipping sound. She came up beside me and started waving.

"Bo, you've come just in time. I'm so glad to see you," she said, squeezing my arm.

Bo grinned back at us, and I was suddenly glad to leave this spot, even if we weren't done, even if more clues remained. I didn't want to be a part of any of this, for even as we prepared to leave, an evil stench filled my nostrils, an overpowering smell of burning carnage that filled my psychic senses.

* * *

I stumbled all the way back to the car, though the going was much easier this way, mostly downhill as Bo had promised. The three of us chattered together, and Flo's package burned a hole in my backpack. I was anxious to look at it, but we dared not unwrap it in Bo's presence.

Next thing we knew, the media would be upon us again.

The forest was beautiful, I noticed, in spite of my preoccupation with other matters. The morning sun sent golden shafts of light that almost reached the ground here where the trees grew tall and stately. Giant oaks were joined by maples and tall pines to form hiding places for the woods creatures.

I wondered idly if there were woods spirits here—fairies or elves or nymphs, whatever you call them. I thought I saw movement at the corner of my eye, but when I turned my head, I saw nothing.

"I'll get you guys," I said, turning all around.

"Get us for what?" Isis asked, sounding amused. Bo looked startled.

"I'm just talking out loud. Excuse me. I was looking for the woods spirits."

"What are woods spirits?" Bo asked.

"I'm surprised you haven't seen any if you spend time in the woods. Now I may not have seen them myself, but sometimes I can sense them. They're the nature angels. They take care of the plants and trees and all the woodland creatures," Isis said.

"You mean like fairies?" Bo asked, scratching his head. "I thought that was all cartoon stuff. None of that's real."

"I believe it is, with all my heart," I said. "One time I went into the forest where there were no other people. It's important to get away from people because they scare them off.

"I found a quiet spot where the sun could hit me and I meditated. I must have meditated for an hour with my eyes closed. Somewhere near the middle of that hour, I felt the nature spirits coming close to me, as if they were curious about me. I could feel them fluttering about me, and they weren't birds, for no bird will come that close.

"When I finally did open my eyes, they were gone, but I knew they had been there; the energy felt delicious and happy when they were around me, fresh as the air after a rain." I felt joy talking about earth's creatures, a by-product of my beliefs.

"Maybe I'll look for them, if you're sure they're real," Bo said.

"They're real," Isis and I said together.

I rejoiced to see the red car, and we all piled in for the short ride back to the motel, Isis at the wheel. When we got back, Bo quickly grabbed his bike and walked it outside.

"Hold up, buddy. Here's something for your help. You're an excellent guide," said Isis, handing Bo a bill.

He opened it out, and his eyes got big.

"Wow, ladies. Thank you, too," he said as if he'd never seen a twenty-dollar bill. Evidently Isis's generosity surpassed that of the news guys.

When he'd gone, we hurriedly packed our things, stowed them in the car, and left our hotel key in the room.

"If we hurry, we can get a quick breakfast at the diner before we head back." I looked at my watch. "It's ten o'clock. We'll just make it in time for my shift at Ruthie's if there are no traffic jams on the way back."

In our haste to eat something and return to the city, Flo's package lay forgotten in my backpack. The diner stretched ahead like an oasis.

Chapter 21

Isis and I talked as we entered the diner, and for once I'd forgotten to examine every last crack in the floor for clues. I felt like my stomach had turned inside out, and I prepared to eat packets of sugar if necessary to survive.

"You realize we accomplished that mission without even so much as a cup of coffee to energize us," I said as a waitress led us to a table near the window. Kim was nowhere in sight.

"You drink that decaffeinated stuff that works by placebo effect, anyway," she said.

The sausages and bacon at a nearby table even looked appetizing, but I stuck to my vegetarian fare of pancakes, scrambled eggs, and home fries. I don't think I lifted my face one time from the plate until I had inhaled every last crumb of food.

I sighed while Isis finished her Belgian waffle with strawberries. We did need to get back to the city posthaste, but that didn't explain why I had gulped my food. The northern air had turned me into a savage.

I looked around the room for the first time since we'd gotten there. Burly men at a large table were standing up and putting their ball caps on.

That's when I saw him.

In the far corner at a small table sat a familiar man. Even with his back to me, I recognized the hand gestures and the way he sat in the chair.

I tried to tell myself I was wrong, but just then he turned our way and I saw the side of his face.

It was Hank.

Panic rose in me full force, not because I feared intimacy with him, but because I had dared to hope we could have a life together.

Across from him at the table sat a woman in her early forties, groomed like the crown princess. A dark beauty, she looked Italian, and the light reflected off her gold neck chains and the diamonds in her ear lobes. Her short, teased black hair framed a face with sensual features. I could see her dreamy, happy expression as she touched him with a hand that glittered with rings on every finger.

Every gesture pointed to the inevitable fact that Hank and this woman must be lovers.

"Look over there," I said in a whisper to Isis.

"You mean those two? Cozy little pair, aren't they? But darling, nobody but nobody teases their hair anymore," Isis said, also lowering her voice.

"I have to get out of here," I said in a strangled voice. "You go ahead and finish. I'll be out at the car."

I threw tip money on the table, grabbed the check, and tried not to look at Isis's startled face. Turning myself so as not to look at Hank and his date, I walked out to the counter, away from the dining room.

I paid our check and heaved a sigh of relief as I charged out the door into the fresh air. This was why I didn't like to get into relationships. No guarantees. I had barely begun with Hank, and here it was over already.

Supercharged by adrenalin, I paced restlessly in the parking lot. Sure enough, Hank's brown and white Bronco sat parked near the back. I hoped and prayed he and his woman wouldn't come out before Isis did.

An emotional confrontation wasn't my style. I just wanted to get out of there.

A few minutes passed before I reentered the earth's atmosphere and started to think again. All of a sudden, the entire focus of this scene shifted. I dropped the "he-done-me-wrong" scenario and instead viewed it through the eyes of a seeker.

What is Hank doing way up here? If he wanted a clandestine romance, he wouldn't have to come this far.

Isis waved as she came toward me now, her face puzzled. "Stephanie, what was that all about?"

"A rude shock, my friend. Can we just get in the car and start driving back? I'll tell you all about it."

I glanced back one last time at the diner as we pulled onto the unpaved road. It was blessedly still—no souls stirring, especially not you-know-who.

"Isis, you won't believe who that was back there."

"Someone important to you from the look of your pale face." Isis shot a worried look my way.

"Remember my customer from the diner that I went out with?"

"You mean Hank? That was Hank at that table in there?"

I nodded. "I see," she said. "Was that his sister?"

"Do you think that was his sister?" My words sounded hoarse as I tried to control my emotions.

"I'm sorry, Stephanie. I'm really sorry. And I encouraged you to get involved with him, too. I'm not sure what he sees in her—she looks pretty artificial. You're a natural beauty. But maybe there's some logical explanation. Maybe this isn't what it seems to be."

We rode in silence for a few minutes. Apple Grove was behind us now in the dust her Dodge kicked up.

"What was Hank doing up here, anyway? This isn't exactly on the way to anywhere," Isis said, having mulled the situation over.

"That's what I've been asking myself. I've only come up with one explanation." I sat with my hands tightly clenched together.

"Can I ask you something important first?"

"Sure," I said.

"Are we going the right way?"

"Yes, dear. I'll tell you when it's time to turn, but for now there's only this unpaved road and you and me." She brought a smile to my face and my heart and I silently thanked her.

"So what's your explanation about Hank being up here?"

"Maybe he's mixed up with this Flo deal somehow." It sounded impossible to my ears, but there weren't any easy answers.

She listened and nodded her head as we drove in the dust. "I guess that could be possible," she said. "But that might make him a bad guy for several reasons, then. He didn't strike me as that type."

"He's not, Isis, but people aren't always who they seem to be." I shivered and tried to calm my short-circuited nerves.

* * *

"I believe strongly in civilization, Moonbeam. That was rough driving back there." We had driven for quite a while and had just hit a two-lane paved road. Isis sighed in relief, then her face lit up. "Aren't we forgetting something?"

"I don't think so. We loaded everything up at the motel before I saw Hank and lost my mind."

"It was truly an exciting find, and we haven't even looked at it yet," she hinted.

"A find—let me see. Oh my gosh, we haven't looked at the bundle Flo left in the tree. I can't believe it."

I rummaged in the back seat to locate my backpack, and then hauled it up front onto my knees. All the sordid thoughts about Hank left my head as I became instantly absorbed in this new project. My hands shook slightly as I pulled the scarf-wrapped object out. Miraculously, the scarf looked dry and intact.

I unwrapped it quickly, revealing a small black volume. I opened it and saw uneven handwriting in black ink.

"Is it what I think it is?" Isis asked.

I didn't even need to look at the cover where she'd written words in white ink. I knew what we had here.

"Yes, Isis, it's Flo's Book of Shadows. If we are to find clues explaining her unnatural death, they'll be in here. I can't believe we found this."

Down through the centuries, the Book of Shadows served as the witch's journal of her rituals and magical activity. Anything of significance in her magical day-to-day life could be recorded, including use of herbs, laying on of hands, the holidays, even recipes.

Certainly anything of spiritual significance would be included in the witch's book.

"It's a pretty small volume. I'd have thought Flo would have had one of encyclopedic proportions," Isis said.

"Evidently, she didn't like to write as well as she liked to talk."

The book was about half filled with entries. I looked at the inside cover where she had written, "My Book of Shadows, Volume Five, begun October 31." It was dated from several years ago and signed "Flo Pohaski."

I opened automatically to an entry that marked the beginning of Flo's split with our group and read silently:

"Isis has great jealousy of my knowledge and expertise in witchcraft. Because of this, she attacked me tonight at Circle. She accused me of negativity and destroying the group's morale. Honestly, those who are great have always had to suffer the abuse of others. That Circle was lucky to have me as a resource person.

"But I can't continue with such an unenlightened woman leading the group. I know the others will suffer from losing me, but it cannot be helped. As long as that woman leads Circle, I will no longer be attending. She isn't just narrow-minded and petty, she's evil."

"What's she writing about?" Isis asked.

"Oh, nothing."

"So she's writing about me."

I looked up and smiled. "She seems to believe in good guys and bad guys, and your name does figure prominently in this section."

I leafed through till the final entry. The handwriting was more uneven here. The last entry was dated December 10, the day before the new moon.

"What a wondrous day! I am finally to be initiated properly into this coven. How they treat me with respect and loving kindness here. They look up to me and ask me for advice. At last I am being shown the proper respect that one of my standing deserves. How intently they listen to me as if each word is a pearl of wisdom.

"I feel cleansed. I feel resurrected. My life here far surpasses anything I've experienced thus far.

"Come along with me, my little Book of Shadows, to witness my moment of triumph. Come along and share these spiritual times together. Come along and register this greatest honor as I join these people of the woodlands."

Flo's grand finale had been imagined to be her greatest triumph. I felt slightly sick as I snapped the book shut.

"Learn anything?" Isis asked quietly, picking up on my mood.

"She calls it a coven, and she thought she was performing some ceremony to join the group. Right to the end, she was out of focus, not really able to see others clearly, to size up the situation.

"She was so obsessed with herself, she couldn't really see or hear anyone else. The price she paid was too great, I think, for her lack of judgment. We'll have to read this closely for clues. Maybe she identified the group and we can find them or turn the information over to the police."

"I doubt it," Isis said.

"I doubt it, too. Her last entry was December 10. I thought you got a letter from her in January."

"Funny thing, I photocopied the envelope, darkened it, and could finally make out the postmark. It was sent in early December."

"Not a very speedy delivery."

"Who knows, Moonbeam? It's a very strange business. But if Flo knew we were studying her secret journal, she might come back and haunt us."

"Now that's something I wouldn't want to miss."

Chapter 22

Home. My little green house sparkled like a palace as I pulled into the driveway. We'd made the trip back in record speed, and I had a half hour to spare to check on my Tricksie.

"Tricksie, I'm home," I called as I burst through the front door.

She appeared from around a corner, her fur ruffled as if she had just wakened, saying "mah." I picked her up and hugged her.

"I'm glad you're all right, Trickster. I don't like to leave you here alone. It seems like I've been gone a month instead of just a day."

My answering machine light was flashing, so I sat on the bed and pushed the play button. Tricksie nestled down beside me. One message—only one person in the whole wide world had thought of me in the past twenty-four hours, at least enough to give me a call.

I held my breath in anticipation, hoping somehow that it was Hank, that I was wrong about him. I should have known better.

"Stephanie, I was just wondering if you'd come home yet. I've got a rain check for a date with you. Maybe tonight? Give me a call on my cell and we'll make plans. I miss your smiling eyes."

It was Alex, and I felt tremendous relief to hear from him. As usual, he was timely.

I needed to forget about Hank.

I pushed the buttons of my cordless, punching in his cell phone number. It rang exactly twice before he answered it.

"Hello, my friend. I'm back from my travels. How are you?"

"Much better now that you're back. Want to go to dinner tonight?"

"I'd like to, but I'm working this evening. I won't get off until eleven."

"We don't have to do dinner, Steph. I just want to let you know what a nice guy I am. We could just go out for some drinks. I can pick you up after work."

I only hesitated a heartbeat.

"That will be great. I missed you." The needy part of me was emerging like a moth from its cocoon. I was hurting so badly. I'd been alone so long I'd forgotten how it felt to hurt, but it all came soaring back to me now.

"I'll be there around eleven, then," he said and rang off.

He sounded excited, but I told myself I was imagining it. I always got the feeling I was a hobby with Alex, his latest fancy to shoo away the clutches of boredom.

"Please forgive me, Tricksie," I said as I pulled on a turquoise top and my black pants. I thought about grabbing another outfit to impress Alex, but decided against it.

I didn't want to appear too eager to impress him.

Tricksie sat on the floor batting a catnip mouse when I lifted her up and hugged her again.

"I don't want to leave, but I'll be back soon," I said to her, hoping it was true. She was now lying on her back, wiggling and chewing on the mouse as I stepped away.

"Oh, maybe I should just stick with cats and their feline ways and forget all about men," I told the air and whoever else might be listening.

I remembered to feed her, brushed the cat hair off the front of my blouse, grabbed my purse, and headed back out to the car.

* * *

That night at the diner was unusually busy. We not only got families, but large families taking up two and three tables. Scruffy-looking workmen still wearing their dirty coveralls sat amongst elderly couples just out for a drive and a bite to eat.

It felt like assembly line waitressing, which I usually detested. Busy, but not crazy busy was always my motto. But tonight being too busy was just about right. Too many memories tried to flood back, and I hadn't expected this emotional avalanche.

There was the table where Hank and I sometimes sat together, about the same size table as the one he'd sat at with that other woman, the one with the fat hair. I tried not to look at "our" table, but it was hard not to, since I'd been assigned that section of the diner.

When I took my break, a short one at that, I stepped out back behind the diner. I saw my favorite pair of cardinals winging themselves into the pine trees and heard their familiar "chit, chit." For some reason, that comforted me.

I wondered how Isis was coming along with Flo's Book of Shadows. We'd decided she was the logical one to study it first. She'd promised to call me if she came upon anything important or enlightening.

I shoved all the Hank thoughts into the back room of my mind, except that when I was here at the diner I couldn't escape one fact: Hank might show up. That reality kept filtering through my mind all night, and I couldn't decide if I wanted him to come in or never wanted to see him again.

Alex, I would tell myself each time my insecurities and Hank's name surfaced. I substituted thoughts of Alex for thoughts of Hank, whether this showed wisdom or not.

The shift passed quickly, slowing down at the very end, a tapering away of my labors. I almost wished I'd brought the change of clothes, except that dressing up wasn't really in my vocabulary or closet, either. Plus Alex arrived so promptly that I wouldn't have had time to change, anyway.

He grinned at me with eagerness.

"Are you ready, my dear Stephanie, for an evening of worldly pleasure? Are you willing to strip away the veneer of everyday life to see what lies beneath?"

"I thought we were going out for drinks," I said, a hint of laughter in my voice.

"Oh, things aren't always what they seem to be. At least admit I am helping you leave your life of toil and enjoy some luxury for a few hours," he said.

"I'm ready. I just need to grab my purse, and then I'll be ready to leave this life of toil."

I followed him to his black Cadillac sport utility vehicle, and he held the door for me. I hadn't the heart to tell him door opening went out the year I had my senior prom. Limo drivers were the only ones who practiced this custom any more.

He hopped in beside me, started the engine, and all the dash lights provided a romantic atmosphere. Come to think of it, K-Mart had seemed air-brushed and inviting that day we'd first run into each other.

"Tell me, shall we go to your place or mine?" he asked, still grinning.

"I haven't been home much. Let's go to my place," I said, not believing my own words.

"I was just joking."

"I wasn't."

I knew what was happening, and I didn't approve of my actions. I wanted to obliterate all thoughts of Hank from my mind until I didn't care anymore. As far as the consequences of being intimate with someone I barely knew—I guess I'd think about that later.

"You really want to go to your place?" he asked, eyebrows raised.

“Yes, I’d like that. I’m not in the mood for a noisy, smoky place.” I gave him directions to my house and I felt the happiest I had in over twenty-four hours.

“Say, what about the mission?” he asked.

“What mission?”

“You know, you went with your friend to see the sick friend? How’d that go?”

“I barely made it back for work, just checked in at the house with my cat, then was off to the diner. Her friend was even sicker than we thought. She’s not expected to make it. There wasn’t much we could do, but I’m still glad we went.”

“So where was it you went, anyway?” His voice sounded casual, but I got a strange feeling about it. I still wanted to keep the details a secret. I didn’t know if I would ever trust Alex completely.

“I didn’t pay much attention, but it was just a small town in a rural area. After a while, they all look the same to me.”

When we pulled in the driveway, I suddenly wished I’d driven my car. I’d truly be home, then. And I wished I was alone, too, for I was suddenly more tired than I thought. I guessed I was emotionally exhausted.

“Please come in, Alex. What can I get you to drink?”

We went through a variety of orders—gin, bourbon, and vodka—until we settled on white zinfandel, which was all I kept in the house.

“You must not have many parties,” Alex said at discovering my nearly liquorless state.

"I don't have any friends, just the people I work with. If I held a party, no one would come."

"You do yourself a great disservice, talking that way. A handsome woman such as yourself could attract all manner of admirers and have plenty of female friends, too."

We sat on my mauve brocade couch sipping from our wine glasses. Tricksie rolled around on the floor beside the glass coffee table.

"I didn't think girls were handsome. I thought that was reserved for men or elderly ladies or pedigreed dogs," I said in amusement. Alex always entertained me.

"Ah, but that's where you're wrong, my handsome friend. Pretty girls can be cute and fluffy, but as the years pass they require more and more makeup and surgical procedures to keep up the illusion. Of course, a truly beautiful woman may stay that way to the end.

"But a handsome woman ages finely so that each wrinkle, every character line only contributes to her attractiveness. No matter what age or stage of life she's in, she glows. She may not be beautiful, but she's fascinating instead. That is the allure of a handsome woman." As he spoke he'd placed the hand without the glass on my knee.

I welcomed his touch, as I welcomed his attentions this night.

"Alex, would you like to hear some music?" I asked. He nodded, and I put on a CD of sultry, sexy songs.

He smiled as the music filled the room. "Do you want to dance, Stephanie?"

We met in the center of the living room floor. Tricksie had the good sense to move to the couch, where she tossed and chewed on a bone-shaped catnip toy. He held me very near, and I felt intoxicated by the warmth of his body, the sensation of his hand on my back. I couldn't blame the wine, for I'd only sipped at it.

We started singing the lyrics together, laughing and dancing like well-seasoned partners. We fit together so nicely as we traveled about the living room.

"You don't have to go if you don't want to," I told him as our dance ended.

"You're amazing me tonight, woman. I didn't expect any of this. I thought we were just going out for a few drinks. I wasn't even sure if you'd want to see me." His face mirrored the surprise in his speech.

"And let me tell you, I'm pretty accurate at reading women." He caught himself and stopped. "Forgive my babbling, dear. Of course, I'll stay."

Chapter 23

The following morning, I woke up by inches, blindly reaching for my Tricksie, but she wasn't anywhere on my bed. The covers beside me were thrown back and crumpled. Then I remembered—Alex had been here.

I stretched and felt new energies flowing through my body. Yes, I felt relaxed this morning—relaxed, yet energized and happy enough to sing like one of the birds outside.

Alex had been a wonderful lover. Scenes ran through my mind—how he had been tender, yet strong. Time had vanished altogether, and there was nothing in this universe but Alex and me.

Nothing else mattered.

We had laughed during our lovemaking, fell asleep, then made love some more. After a time, I didn't know if I was awake or dreaming, but it didn't matter, for as long as it went on, I was happy.

Yet again, I was reminded that Alex and I were far from strangers. That strong feeling interlaced our night together—that we had been lovers in another time and place. I couldn't remember being with him before, but the idea nagged at me, and I wanted to know its origin.

Who had Alex been to me before?

Yet the energies flowed between us as fiery, volcanic bursts into the sky. My most exciting partner of all time, he elevated lovemaking onto a new consciousness. Maybe my memory failed me; after all, it had been several years since I'd been with a man.

"Do you have any shaving cream, Steph?" Alex stood just inside the bedroom holding my razor. He looked wide awake, and I resisted the urge to hug him.

"I just use liquid hand soap in there. It's nice to see you this morning. Do you have to rush off?"

He fingered his beard stubble as if it were broken glass.

"Guess I'll have to run home to the apartment. I don't think liquid hand soap will work on my beard. Of course I would have liked to spend the morning with you, my gorgeous lady, but I have some meetings. Can't be late."

He emerged in a few minutes and pulled on his clothes of the night before, looking slightly crumpled.

I had to ask him. I couldn't wait a minute longer.

"Just one thing, Alex. Last night when we made love, it felt as though we had been together before, perhaps in a former lifetime. It all felt so familiar and it flowed so wonderfully. Did you experience any feelings like that?" I felt my heart thumping as if I feared his answer.

He looked up at me without smiling, his eyes searching my face.

"Funny you should say that. Yes, it did seem like that to me, too. It was as if we were one person, not two. Your body felt familiar to me as I explored each part. Maybe that's it. Maybe we've been together before," he said.

"I wonder," I said.

"But I'm more concerned about the future than the past. I hope we'll have repeat performances. After all, we need to study this phenomenon further."

We kissed—a tender, lingering one—and then he straightened his clothes.

"I've got to get home before Alice leaves," he said with a smile.

"Who's Alice?" I asked, little prickles of alarm raising the hairs on the back of my neck. Not again, I thought.

"Didn't I tell you about Alice? She's my roommate."

"How long?" Warning bells gonged in my brain.

"Sixteen years. Every year I think she'll throw me out, but she hasn't done that yet."

"So she's like a wife?"

"Oh, no, we're not married. She's more like a best girlfriend." His smile dazzled, but my heart sank, my shackles rose.

"Isn't it common law marriage after seven years?"

"She spends the summers on Cape May without me, so that's how we get around that."

Words failed me now, so that I wanted to rush into the closet and start a new life there. My face felt hot, and mental confusion swirled like a tornado in my head.

Out of the frying pan, into a bonfire.

"Anything wrong?" he said in genuine concern and hovered over me.

"I just didn't know about the girlfriend."

"Does it matter? It doesn't change the physical side of our relationship. That was great." His black eyes gleamed.

"I'll need to think about it. I've been getting a few surprises lately."

He kissed me on the forehead.

"We'll just have some fun, Stephanie. Keep it light and trivial. Nobody gets hurt this way."

He turned and walked to the door, and I let him go. I heard the door open and close, and then the sound of his big Cadillac starting up.

Nobody gets hurt—speak for yourself, buddy. I waited numbly until I knew he was gone, and then dived back under my covers.

I heard her purring, her small feet padding over me, so I reached a hand out from the depths of the bedclothes. Her fur felt soft and fluffy as baby's hair.

"This only proves one thing, Tricksie." I could hear the loud, resonant purring and feel the paws kneading the covers. "In the future I will renounce all men and stick to loving you."

"Mah," she said with great knowing.

* * *

I didn't want to ever get up again, just obliterate myself somehow, but the phone rang insistently until the answering machine kicked in, and I heard Isis leaving a message.

I grabbed the receiver.

"Isis, this is me. I'm not completely awake yet. What time is it, anyway?"

"You sound a little fuzzy. It's about 9:30. You're usually wide awake by now."

"I was up part of the night." The less said, the better. My brain started to function enough that I guessed the reason for her call. "Did you find anything in Flo's Book of Shadows?"

"That's what I wanted to show you. Can you come over and take a look at it with me? I think there's some important stuff in here."

"I have to get myself going first, feed the cat. All right if I come over in an hour or an hour and a half?"

"That will be great, Moonbeam. I want to make sure I'm interpreting it right. See you when you get here."

Another pang of guilt grabbed me. I knew Tricksie enjoyed my company, and I hated to leave her alone again. "That's it, Tricks. I'll be home tonight after work and tomorrow morning. You can count on that." I patted her soft fur with real regret.

I did my chores and got ready for work, then stepped through the door into my one-car garage and the emptiness echoed through the room.

Where was my ancient Escort? Then I remembered how I had crawled into the Cadillac and come home with Alex.

Muttering to myself, something about no men and only cats from now on, I stepped next door, hoping my neighbor was home. He answered after the first few knocks.

"Whatever you're selling, I already have too much of it already. Oh, it's you, Stephanie. I'll bet you're selling Girl Scout cookies again this year. I'll take two of the thin mints."

He held his screen door open, every dark hair in place, his blue eyes shining behind dark-rimmed glasses. Tony rarely made serious comments.

"Tony, I wish I were taking orders. I'm in a jam right now. I need to go somewhere and my car isn't here." I hoped he wouldn't ask too many questions, and I wondered if he'd spied Alex's SUV last night.

"Did it run away from home, or drive away, I suppose?"

"It's over at the diner, but I'm here, so I need a ride over. If you do, I'll see you get the thin mints."

"I'd do almost anything for thin mints and for Girl Scouts such as you. Let me grab the keys to the Jeep and we'll ramble on over to Ruthie's." He disappeared for a minute, reappeared, and put his arm around me, ushering me out to the teal Wrangler.

"At least you remembered where you live. Things could have been a lot worse," he said.

Tony chatted on cheerfully during the ten-minute drive to the diner, and I stole a look at his profile. An attractive man, he seemed to be enjoying our impromptu date. He almost looked sad when we reached Ruthie's.

"Oh, perhaps you drove it home last night, but it got lonely for the diner and came back by itself."

"Thank you, Tony. You're a lifesaver," I said, then stepped out of the Jeep.

"At your service, Ms. Scout," he said, waved, and pulled away.

I inhaled deeply. Tony was fun, attractive, and about my age. I often wondered why we never connected.

He was probably too wholesome.

Besides, he made a great neighbor. I reached into my jeans pocket for my car keys, made for the Escort, then stopped. Parked right beside my car was the brown and white Bronco.

Hank's Bronco.

Road blocks loomed everywhere this morning. Maybe I wasn't meant to visit Isis right now. One obstacle after another appeared out of nowhere.

I glanced at my watch and knew I still had plenty of time to get to Deborah's before work. I opened the car door and tossed in a bag with my work outfit. I stood an extra second composing myself, asking for help in dealing with this situation.

Then the ridiculous aspect of this morning struck me. Hank had seen my car, but I wasn't in the diner anywhere. I began to laugh—a quiet, hysterical laugh. Hank was in trouble, but it looked like I was, too.

Everybody had explaining to do.

My steps unsteady, I reluctantly walked into Ruthie's.

Chapter 24

He sat at the counter talking with Rosemary, who filled his coffee cup. She nodded toward me and he half turned around to greet me when I got to them. I felt warmth toward him, despite my reservations and the questions that poisoned my thoughts.

"Thought I'd stop a second to say hello, Hank. I'm on my way to visit a friend right now." Feelings bubbled up from my depths, but I couldn't stop to figure them out right now.

"Hello, Stephanie. I stopped because your car was parked here, then we couldn't locate you," Hank said, looking masculine and gorgeous.

"And I stopped in because I saw your Bronco. Did you have a good vacation?" I decided to avoid the issue of my Escort and me.

"The vacation went very well. Thank you for asking." His smile looked a trifle fixed on his face.

I froze as I realized he hadn't seen me in the diner in the mountains. He had no idea I'd seen him with some other adoring woman, and I wasn't sure what to do. My policy has always been if you don't know what to do, then do nothing.

I heaved a sigh. I'd so wanted to clear up this mess. Yet now I had my own mess to clean up.

"Where are you? You've gone somewhere," Hank said, staring strangely into my face.

"I'm right here. Things have changed since you went away. But I need to get going or my friend will come looking for me."

"Is he anyone I know?" Hank asked with care.

"His name is Deborah, and I don't think so. I thought you saw me with her once, but I was mistaken."

"Is everything all right between you and me?" he asked. "You're talking in riddles today."

"Some things need explained. I'll tell you later, Hank. We'll get it straightened out. I've got to run over to Deborah's, then come back and work tonight."

"We'll talk next time, then. I shouldn't be going away any time soon. I was thinking about asking you out right away, but I guess that can wait until later. Would that be best?"

I gulped and nodded, both wanting and not wanting to see him. Avoiding conflict ranked high on my list of things to do.

"Great to see you," he said.

I wanted to say "glad you're back," but it stuck in my throat. I wanted to trust him and love him, but I couldn't even trust myself. This was a love rectangle I didn't wish to be involved in.

Whatever happened to happily-ever-after?

"I'll see you later, Hank. Take care."

"I'll see you tomorrow. You'll be here, won't you?" The puzzled look on his face made me catch my breath.

I'd left the counter, but came back and put a hand on his broad shoulder. "I'll be here. Sorry I'm not right today. See you tomorrow."

I escaped the diner feeling guilty and strongly attracted to Hank, wondering if he had some plausible explanation for his up north activities, wondering if I wanted to see Alex again.

The car started right up, just like always, and I pulled away, pointed east with my many questions and not one answer to lighten my load.

* * *

She answered the door on the first ring with a French braid and flowers in her hair, perfectly complementing her pink shirt and flowered tight pants.

"Come in, Moonbeam. I think you're going to be excited by this information. It's almost as if Flo left this behind for us to find."

After a brief hug, which I needed after my shaky morning, I followed her to the kitchen with its dark purple cabinets—a spiritual space if I'd ever seen one.

"Please have a seat," she said. "I have the spot marked in the journal."

I slid into a wooden chair and picked up the Book of Shadows. It felt heavier this time, and I sensed a darkness about it—a denseness or negativity. It didn't feel joyful and light the way my journal always did to me.

I opened it to the page Isis had marked with a Star Trek bookmark. Captain Picard looked wise as ever and I wondered if he'd explored the new worlds I'd encountered in the past few days.

The same uneven handwriting caught my eye.

"Begin on the left-hand entry and read on," Isis said, pointing to the page.

I nodded and began. I became so absorbed in the writing that when Isis set a steaming cup of herbal tea by me, I barely even noticed it.

I read until the words began to blur. I looked up at her and felt her concern. These paragraphs, these pages were full of emotional impact. I felt it in my chest—heaviness, an aching caused by the secrets revealed in Flo's journal.

"Do you think it's true?" I asked Isis, hoping these pages were wrong.

"I've meditated about this since I read Flo's entries. I'm fairly sure her conclusions are accurate."

A shiver rocked my body. I wanted to toss this book into the ocean from a high cliff. Instead, I closed it, set it down, and then sipped at the tea.

"Can you talk about it?" Isis asked from a chair opposite me.

"I guess we'd better talk about it. I won't be able to sleep otherwise. I just can't believe it."

"I know. It hit me hard, too. And to think, she's spent six years in this group."

"Driving us crazy," I said with a cockeyed smile, "but it's a very short drive."

"That's a lot better than what she did before—and I do think it's true."

"Let's see if we read the same thing. Is she really saying that she and most of us from Circle lived during the Burning Times?" I still couldn't believe what I had read.

"That's right. She meditated and received the information. She meditated about the group because she knew something was wrong. It was her attempt to solve the problems she brought to the group," Isis said.

"She thought by meditating she could somehow change you, Isis. She assumed you were the real problem. How like her."

"The meditating, in turn, brought her dreams, and she saw visions while she meditated. She insists nearly all Circle members were present during the Burning Times."

"And we all burned. That part doesn't surprise me, especially since I had the vision at Samhain. Even before that, I had vague notions about that, nothing definite," I said.

"Me, too. I've had a few dreams about that myself. But this is now and that was then. I didn't think it related to the present time."

"Flo writes here that she was the only one who wasn't burned. She turned us in to some religious figure who gave our names to the authorities."

"She says later that we were raided during a ritual. We were grabbed in the woods at night. Next thing you know, we were crispy critters. Flo didn't attend the ritual that night—said she was sick."

The significance of all this filtered through to me.

"This must be some kind of karmic event, Flo being burned to death in the woods. She engineered our deaths by burning, then dies by the same method. Only we had nothing to do with it," I said.

"I have more to read of her journal, but I haven't yet come upon a motive and the people who did her in. I don't know why she turned us in back then, but we may never know that one. At least we learned one thing—her death in the woods is more complicated than it looks from the surface."

"And one more thing, Isis."

"Yes?"

"Flo never was our friend. She was a dark influence from centuries ago."

We both shivered, and after nervous laughter, Isis promised to keep in touch with any more information that came to light.

"I'll be calling you, too," I said. "But for now I'd better hustle back over to the diner for another exciting evening of shuffling burgers and fries to my public."

"Did he show up?" she asked, clearly remembering our Apple Grove adventure.

"You mean Hank?" She nodded, and I sighed. "Yes he did, and he acts as if he didn't see us. It's as if nothing has happened."

“Sounds like the next move is up to you. You might want to ask him a few questions.”

“Especially since he was supposed to be on vacation taking care of family business,” I said.

“I don’t think that woman was his mother.”

I smiled awkwardly and rose to leave and felt the tight throat and face that preceded tears. “I’m going to wait till I get his story. It could all be a big misunderstanding.”

Isis nodded her head, but I could sense suspicion filling her energy fields and her physical body. She thought Hank was a bad guy, sent to the diner to hurt me.

Not this time. I stubbornly held to my beliefs. *Not my friend Hank.*

Chapter 25

A week later, I awoke gasping for air, as if I had been down beneath the surface of a lake, down there waiting until my lungs nearly burst. I sweated profusely, adding to the lake effect, my hair drenched and clinging to my head. I sat up in bed panting, returning to this time and place.

I had been there again, back to the Burning Times, I was sure of it. I viewed an ancient forest, the trees gnarled and venerable. I sensed the others with me—other women. We were all women.

I could feel the flames, dancing high now. We laughed, drank ale, and ate cakes around our circle, much as we do today. But this wasn't now, this was far back in time, and we celebrated in some forest unknown to me now.

Then the screaming began; I heard screaming and motion around me. My friends were running. I tried to get up, but something was weighing me down, and I felt relief amidst the fear, amidst the fleeing.

I surfaced from the dream, glad to be back here, away from that strange, yet familiar existence. Back here where I was safe.

Or was I?

Tricksie consoled me, rubbing against my sweaty limbs, crying softly to bring me back.

"I'm not sure I want to pursue this Flo Pohaski mystery any further," I said to her, brushing her lightly with sweaty palms, as if she understood my words. "Everything has been going downhill since she disappeared."

I wiped myself with the sheet, and thought how my nice, comfortable life of service to others was disintegrating against my will. Now I had become involved with two men, and my roots as a witch turned rancid right beneath my nose.

I had had two more passionate dates with Alex in the past week. Had I wanted to be with him? I wasn't sure, but the lovemaking was exquisite. He took me places I had never been before, but when he left, I crashed. He went home to his woman, and I was left with my cat wondering what it was all about.

I supposed it had more to do with running away from Hank.

Hank—I always felt warm when I thought of him, even now when he'd become a traitor. Yes, I suppose I was running away from Hank, but I had nowhere real to run to.

Hank and I had seen each other nearly every day at the diner in the past week, yet our relations were formal, stiff. I had little time to spend with him, being legitimately busy at my work.

The question burning me up was: Who was that dark-haired woman and why were you in Apple Grove, Hank? But so far I couldn't ask it. I guess I feared bad news, having my worst fears confirmed. It was silly, really, holding back this way. Yet Alex stood between us now in some strange way—Alex who didn't want me, who was just keeping it light. At least Hank had seemed to want something more.

I shivered, a cool breeze reaching me from somewhere in the room; Tricksie bolted, jumping onto the floor. "I have to stop thinking about this stuff. I'm driving myself crazy. It's all going round in circles, like a merry-go-round, and I want to get off."

I got up and moved toward the shower. I felt cleansed as the warm water beat against my skin. I visualized all my troubles washing off me, out of me, down into the drain.

I toweled off, appreciating the warmth of the towel. As I brushed my hair, untangling what had been sweaty but now smelled of lavender shampoo, I relaxed. This was my day off. There were hours to wile away, time to lavish attention on Tricksie.

The phone rang, probably another long distance carrier harassing me. I picked up, said hello, and waited for the long pause that signified I could hang up and avoid harassment.

"It's big news this time," she said.

"Isis?" My heart thumped already.

"Who else calls you up and harasses you?"

"The telemarketers. You don't harass me. What's this big news?"

"I got a call from friendly Ralph from Apple Grove."

"Ralph? How did he get your number?"

"Remember? I left a business card with him. I like to think ahead."

"Was he asking you out? He was pretty taken with you as I recall."

"No romance. He had a news tip for us. Said he wasn't going to contact the news media, but he thought we might want to know. It's about Flo's coven."

I felt myself getting excited. The invisible coven was finally going to materialize.

"What did he say?" I asked.

"It's his niece. A teenager. She and a few of her friends had contact with this coven. Evidently, it was a traumatic experience."

"So they have information for us. Didn't they contact the local police?"

"No police, Moonbeam. No police and no news media. We have an exclusive on this story. This is only because Ralph has the hots for me. And he thinks we can somehow help these girls.

"And there's one other thing, a reference in Flo's diary to the coven. She gives a little information which we can correlate with these girls."

"We? Correlate? What are you suggesting, Isis?" My stomach felt queasy.

"I thought maybe we could run up there and do some investigating."

"When?"

"As soon as possible. In the next few days while these girls are still willing to talk. When could you go?"

"I only have today off, then I'll be working a stretch of five or six days." I felt a sinking sensation as I realized my luxurious day with Tricksie was disappearing.

"Can you go today? I don't have anything big, just one appointment I can reschedule. This would be an up and back trip, no staying at their five star motel."

All this Flo business came crashing down around me, and my gut told me to stay home, get a life, let Flo's demise fade away until no one cared any more. I wanted to decline, but basic loyalty to Isis made me go against my better judgment.

"Sure, I can meet you in Greentree in about an hour. Would that work?"

"Perfect."

* * *

Isis insisted on driving again, so I read Flo's journal entries regarding her new coven. The information had been hard to track down, for it was tucked away amidst recipes for herbal teas, rum punch, and breads with herbs in them.

"So she made her contact with this group in Pittsburgh. That makes sense. I can't see her running all the way up here to be with nature," I said.

"She answered an ad in one of those free newspapers, *Pittsburgh Life*. The ad vaguely referred to witchcraft, and she suspected it was a coven."

"She doesn't give any names or descriptions so that we could identify this group. She only says a man and woman are leaders. She mostly focuses on how important she is to this group. She's an elder, or crone, and is looked up to."

Isis gave me a glance above her glasses. "They only knew her a few months. And then they murdered her. I'd say our group was more loving."

"Flo was out of balance, unable to see the big picture. You were always extremely patient with her, Isis. Is there anything more in here I should read?"

"I don't think so, at least not now. I may have missed something, but I tried to look it all over. She talks a lot about physical symptoms—headaches, sinus trouble, bloating, and her bowels—I had to skim over some of that."

I snapped the Book of Shadows shut and gratefully tossed it into the back seat. I didn't enjoy prying into Flo's journal. I didn't even like touching it, as if her strange energies clung to the book, contaminating my energy fields when I held it.

"How long till we get there, Moonbeam?" my driver asked with amusement.

"If you're good and we don't make many stops, it could be as early as the second Tuesday of next week."

She stuck her tongue out at me, and we settled into a companionable silence.

Chapter 26

This time the miles flew by and we pulled onto the unpaved road before we knew it. In a few minutes, I could see the familiar buildings of Apple Grove in the distance.

"It only took us three hours and fifteen minutes this time, but it seemed like about an hour. We got here in no time at all," I said.

"Gee, maybe we could come up here every weekend for a vacation retreat hide-away," Isis said.

"I wouldn't get carried away with the idea. Just because the trip went well doesn't mean I want to be here."

"Didn't you want to come?" Isis turned suddenly serious as she pulled into the post office and garage lot. Ralph was nowhere in sight.

"I didn't want you to come by yourself, friend. As for me, my orderly life has transformed to turmoil since we started pursuing the Flo mystery. But I'm not complaining. Maybe it would have anyway."

"But you wouldn't have known about Hank and whoever else in Apple Grove if we hadn't come here. I'm sorry, Stephanie."

"My therapist used to say you can deny reality, but in the end reality always wins. I guess I'd rather know than not know. Shall we go in?"

We hadn't made one stop in our cruise up to the northlands. The roads were mercifully clear and in our excitement, none had been necessary. Now we nosed into the garage, which was deserted. Isis looked uneasy until we stepped through the front door of the post office.

He looked cleaned up this time. His ponytail hung neatly down his back, and his eyes lit up when they rested on Isis. It was as if I wasn't even there.

"Miss Deborah. I didn't expect you to make it so quickly. What a nice surprise. Can I offer you and your friend a drink?" He nodded in my direction.

She looked at me and I smiled. We didn't even have to discuss it. "What we need more than anything is a bathroom," she said.

"Right this way." He ushered us behind the counter to a door marked "for employees only" and we each took a turn.

He was sorting mail when we returned, but in a haphazard fashion, as if his mind was preoccupied by important thoughts.

"I suppose you'd like to talk to the girls. Are you sure you don't want lunch or something to eat before we start out? I'd be glad to treat you gorgeous ladies," Ralph said. This time I felt included.

We conferred and agreed hunger wasn't a problem; we wanted to move right ahead to the investigation. "We'll pass on lunch. Since we're just here for the day, we'd like to talk to the girls right away. I hope this won't interrupt your work," Isis said.

"This isn't a very bustling metropolis, or have you noticed? I can knock off for an hour or two and nobody even knows." He finished sorting the mail and picked up the phone.

"I'll just call over there and make sure she's there." Ralph talked briefly, then returned the receiver to the white wall phone. "Let's go."

We followed him outside and watched him flip over an "Out to lunch" sign on the post office door.

"I can drive," Isis offered.

"Oh, no, you've done enough driving just to get here. Please allow me," Ralph said. His routine was starting to get to me. "We've a storm coming in tonight, but you ladies should be all right."

He led us to a metallic blue sport utility vehicle, a Grand Cherokee. Its exterior was shiny and spotless, matching the cleaned-up Ralph better than the former Ralph in mechanic's clothes.

"Four-wheel drive is a must up here where the roads are bad even in the summer. It won't take us long to get there." He turned on the engine and drove up the road past the motel and diner.

I couldn't help but examine the diner's parking lot for familiar vehicles. I sighed in relief when I couldn't find the cream and brown Bronco.

Hank wasn't there.

Isis and Ralph talked as I watched the scenery go by—acres and acres of trees on either side of us. We passed over a small bridge with a happily bubbling stream beneath it. We'd come along about ten minutes when Ralph turned left onto a dirt track.

We saw only an occasional house trailer now. When Ralph turned off the dirt road onto another dirt road, I felt slightly anxious.

"We're really getting out in the sticks," I said.

"Don't worry. I've lived here all my life. I know these back roads, and it's impossible for me to get lost," Ralph said, who caught my drift.

I sulked, suddenly overcome by all this great wilderness. We hadn't passed a single business on these roads, and I began to get lonely for a Dairy Queen or a department store.

We climbed a big hill, and then turned into a lane that had been paved. I felt like we had reached civilization again, especially since a large, modern dark log cabin lay at the end of this drive. The house had a two-car garage, a big front porch, and a fountain in front.

Ralph parked in front of the garage, and we stepped down and followed him. He rapped at the front door, explaining as he did, "This is my brother's place. He's the prosperous one in the family—moved to the city and made a lot of money. This is his weekend retreat place. By the way, when you were here before, I didn't know about my niece's connection with this group. I just found out."

A small girl answered the door, her hair blonde but obviously bleached, a straw-like fluff. She stood slight and waif-like, her brown eyes circled in mascara, lashes heavy with it. She held the door wide open, and I noticed a rose tattoo on her right shoulder, a colorful dragon on her left forearm, a studded leather dog collar around her neck, silver earrings up and down each ear, and rings in her nose and right eyebrow.

I shivered and wondered what else lurked beneath her black jeans and black skin-tight top.

"Hi, Raven," Ralph said. "These are the ladies I was telling you about. Deborah, Stephanie, this is my niece Raven."

"Come in. Thanks for making the trip," Raven said.

I was struck by her presence. She must have been sixteen or seventeen, yet she seemed more experienced than her years, certainly not a child.

"Let's go into the living room," she said, motioning to the flowered couch and forest green chairs. I scanned the interior of the house and approved of the light walls, colorful fabrics, and glass and lights.

"I haven't wanted to talk about any of this, but if it will help you ladies, I'm willing to answer questions. Ralph thinks a lot of you, and he thinks talking to you will help me, too. I've been trying to put it all behind me. It all seems like a nightmare now," Raven said, looking small and lost, the brown eyes mellow and sad.

"We only want you to talk about this if it's comfortable for you," Isis said, and I knew she was sincere. "Sometimes, if you hold in your emotions, your pain, it can hold you back. It blocks your energy and can even create physical illnesses. A therapist might be a good idea to work through these issues."

“My parents aren’t big on therapists. They want to keep the whole thing quiet. They think I’m some kind of freak,” Raven said.

“We don’t think you’re a freak,” Isis said. I looked from Isis’s gold nose ring to Raven’s silver one. “I hope sincerely that if you want help, you seek it out and find it. You mustn’t bury this trauma. But for now, Stephanie and I offer our ears to you. Can you tell us what exactly has happened to you?”

“And you promise not to tell anyone else about this? Or I can’t talk.”

“We’ll keep it all confidential, like we’re therapists.”

Raven sighed and said, “I got mixed up with bad, bad people. By the time I figured that out, it was too late.” She stopped as if she could go no further, an odd little smile about her lips.

“How did you come in contact with these people?” I asked.

“There were three of us—me and my friends Julie and Andrea. We go to school together, and sometimes on the weekend Julie and Andrea would come with us here.

“But we didn’t learn about this here in the mountains. Andrea told us about it. She’d been reading books about witchcraft, and she got excited about it. Have you heard much about it?”

Isis and I grinned and glanced at each other.

“We belong to the Women’s Healing Circle in Pittsburgh. We explore the Goddess energy and observe rituals as a group. We like to think we’re witches,” Isis said.

"That's great," Raven said as her eyes widened. "If we had only known you then. We could have avoided a lot of pain and trouble."

"I knew you two were special. I just couldn't put my finger on it. I've never met a witch before," Ralph said with great reverence written into his features.

"Thank you, Ralph," Isis said. "Our group has provided me with much help and inspiration; it's given me the mission for my life. I'm sure Stephanie agrees with me."

I nodded. "But back to Andrea and her studies. What happened next, Raven?" I asked.

"She said she'd met some witches and she wanted us to meet them, too." Raven shifted in the forest green chair.

"How did she meet them?" Isis asked.

"She read an ad in *Pittsburgh Life* about a sacred coven. I never saw the ad, but she called and made contact and thought they were into white witchcraft. We only met them once in the city. Pittsburgh."

"What did you think of them? Who were they?" Isis asked. I could sense her excitement as I felt my own grow.

"I'm still not sure who they were. A couple met us at the mall and took us to their place. I guess that was stupid of us to go, but we were looking for excitement. The lights were off and candles burned throughout the room with just this couple and us there.

"They talked about gaining power through magic. They said their group met and performed rituals in the mountains. Then I found out they met not far from where we are now." Raven's voice drifted off as she ended.

"So did you meet with the group?" I asked gently.

"It was like a big adventure. The couple seemed nice. We were always looking for answers, us and our teenage friends. We didn't like the world of our parents. So we met with the group just a few weeks later. We came up in a black van from Pittsburgh. Others from their group drove up, too. Here I was in this forest that I know and love, excited about these new friends and this new group."

She had been speaking with her eyes cast down, her hands tightly clasped together. Now she looked up, carefully staring each of us in the eyes.

"It was the most disgusting night of my life."

Chapter 27

Raven started crying softly. Ralph got up and came back with a box of tissues, which he gave to her. He leaned down and whispered in her ear, but I could hear him say, "Get it out, baby. Get it all out. We'll get the bastards that did this to you."

I wondered about all this; it felt darker than I'd expected. I shivered, and my whole body shook.

"Are you sure you're ready to talk today? We can come back another time," Isis said. She was being extremely kind and sensitive, but I gritted my teeth. My cat and I weren't fond of these trips to the mountains.

Her crying subsided. Raven blew noisily into the tissue, then looked at us with her reddened eyes and streaked mascara. Ralph excused himself and went outside to wait for us.

"It'll be a long time—maybe never—before this won't be painful any more. So I may as well get it out now." She blew her nose again and began.

"It was last fall when we went. They took us far up into the woods, far away from any locals. I'm sure I could never find the spot again. There seemed to be other new people besides us, also teenagers, but mostly there were people who already belonged to this group.

"We hiked up to a big clearing where wood was laid out for a big fire. There was a wooden platform at one edge of the clearing with an upside down cross attached to it. We were so excited, I suppose we didn't see all that was there.

"As it got dark, our leaders lit the fire. We sat around it, but not close, for it was a fairly warm night in late September. The members of the group put on robes, mostly black, but we wore our jeans and shirts. We all moved over to the platform, which they called an altar.

"The man and woman led us in the ritual, calling upon the powers of darkness. That was when we first suspected something was wrong. Andrea whispered to me that white witches don't call upon the dark powers, only the light.

"The man finally invoked Satan to join our group, and that was when we first realized we'd joined some version of a demonic group. White witchcraft and Black Magic are worlds apart, aren't they?" Raven said.

"Yes, witches work only for the good of themselves and others. That's white magic. Black cults degrade all they touch. I'm not terribly knowledgeable about them, but I've heard their work is evil," Isis said.

"You're right about them; you're absolutely right," Raven said vehemently. "They're dirty, evil people. They maim, hurt, and destroy all they touch. They should be put in jail."

"What happened during their ritual?" I asked and hoped Raven could continue her story.

"The moon was full that night—beautiful, large, and pale. I remember staring at the moon, staring to blot out all the ugliness and the screams.

"They killed small animals. We didn't watch. They were sacrificing them to the Dark Lord. Andrea told me real witches don't even believe in Satan, and they certainly don't kill animals.

"Then a woman in black robe presented a girl about our age to the man and woman—the high priest and priestess. She was a beautiful girl with long, blonde hair. She must have been there before, because she cried and struggled to get away.

"The high priestess said words over her and sprinkled her with water, and then two of the cult members held her while another raped her.

"Andrea, Julie, and I tried to leave. We tried running in the dark beyond the ritual space, but men came after us and caught us. They brought us back and tied our hands behind our backs. Just as we suspected, we were next in the ritual. The high priestess ripped our clothing off and one by one, the three of us were raped.

"I didn't watch; it may have been the high priest, it may have been one of the others. Then they packed us back in the van and drove us back to the city. And we've never seen or heard from them since. They said if we told they'd murder us or our parents."

"What about the others—Julie and Andrea? Have they talked about their experiences?" Isis asked.

"I don't think so. We three talked about it once. I don't think they told their parents. We were all afraid these people would kill us or our families. I believe they might do it.

"My parents wanted me to talk to the police, but I won't take the chance. I don't want them to find me again. I don't want to see or hear of them again." Raven sat on the couch with her legs folded up in a fetal position. As she talked, she rocked slightly.

"Would you recognize any of them again?" Isis asked.

"It was pretty dark at the ritual site and in the van. The only ones we saw were the man and woman."

"Would you recognize them again?"

"Yes, I think so, though they usually wore robes with their hoods up."

"What did they look like?" I felt anticipation as Isis asked this important question.

Raven stared off into space. "The woman was about forty, with dark hair, a nice figure, though maybe a little on the chubby side."

"What was her name?"

"I don't think they ever told us their names. I've tried and tried, but I can't remember. The just said they were the high priest and priestess."

"What did he look like?" I asked.

Raven sighed. "He's even fuzzier in my mind than the woman. Maybe my mind's just blocking him out. He was taller than her, maybe six feet. I can't see his face any more. He had a good build, no fat on him, and he was probably over forty.

"He wore some kind of hat when he didn't have his hood on, so I don't even know what color his hair is. I'm sorry I didn't get their names."

"Chances are they wouldn't have given you their real names anyway," Isis said.

"What about the other people in the group? Did you find out who they were?" I asked.

"We didn't really talk with any of them. They looked like nice people until the ritual began. They could have been anyone."

"But you were at the couple's house. Do you remember where that is?" Isis asked in a sudden inspiration.

"I've tried to find it, but none of us can. It was night, and we went to a part of town none of us knew. Plus we didn't exactly pay attention. We were so busy talking that none of us remembers the outside of the house."

"So the only connection we have to this couple and group is the newspaper ad. You're sure you can't find the place where they held the ritual?" Isis asked.

Raven shook her head. "I've looked for that, too, and I know a lot of places around here. I'm not sure where it was, but I do know one thing for sure."

"What's that?" I asked.

"Uncle Ralph took me to the spot where the poor woman was burned. I'm certain we were in a different location. That looked different—the trees, no platform. I'm thinking this was the same group, and they move the location for each ritual.

"I can't explain it, but when I was looking at the spot, I got the strongest feeling that it was the same group again."

"What about your friends Andrea and Julie?" Isis asked. "Will they talk with us, too?"

"They said no, but they didn't know how nice you are. They wouldn't come over."

"That's all right, Raven, Maybe later they'll want to talk. They can call us at any time. How are you feeling about talking about your experiences?" Isis asked.

A slow, tired smile spread across her face. Now we understood why she seemed older than her years.

"I feel much better, actually. Some of the heaviness is gone." She gestured toward her heart.

"Does your friend still have the ad from the newspaper?" I asked.

"She threw it away. We burned everything at Andrea's house, including the clothes we'd worn. Andrea even burned all her books on witches after that. We were pretty upset."

"Is there anything else you want to talk about or tell us?" I asked.

"Just that I never believed in evil before that. I didn't think it was real. Now I've seen evil and it was uglier than I ever dreamed it would be. How can people be like that?" Raven asked, tears appearing in her eyes again.

I looked at Isis, for her wisdom in these matters was greater than mine.

"All throughout history, my dear Raven, there has been cruelty and injustice. The light has always been with us, but so has been the darkness. I don't begin to understand the darkness, the evil ones of this world. I just know, and I feel it in my being, that the light, the forces of good, far outweigh the forces of evil.

"I am so sorry you got pulled into this group. The light has always attracted the darkness. Somehow you must use this to become stronger, to serve others, to learn yet not be broken by it." Isis spoke softly, yet confidently.

"How do I get my trust back?" Raven asked.

"We could do a ritual to purify you. Have you called the archangels and your guardian angels in to help you?" I asked.

"What kind of ritual?" Raven looked startled.

"Just us women in a circle. Our altar is a cloth on the ground with candles on it. We would use a bundle of burning sage and salt water to purify you, and speak as a group and meditate to heal your body, mind, and spirit. It would be at Friends' Meeting House in Oakland, not up here in the woods," I said.

Raven relaxed visibly as I explained.

"I might like that, and to learn about the angels, too."

“I can send you a book about the angels. Your angels will help you work through the worst of this,” I said, then mentally called forth Archangel Raphael and the healing angels to help Raven with her trauma.

“How else can we help you?” Isis asked.

“That’s enough. You’ve helped so much already. I feel so much better, like I’ve been let out of some prison. I’ll talk to Julie and Andrea. Maybe they’ll want to be in a healing ritual.”

“Just call us about the ritual—if you’re interested, I mean,” Isis said.

“I will.”

We stood up and stretched. Isis and I in turn embraced Raven warmly.

“It was brave of you to share with us. Somehow this will benefit others, we’re sure of it, and you can use healing methods to deal with it,” I said.

We walked out the door onto the large porch. It was a clear, sunny day, and I felt better being outside instantly.

“There’s one thing you might want to pursue, though I never did,” Raven said, looking more energetic already.

“What’s that?” Isis said.

“That newspaper. They shouldn’t be running ads for that group,” Raven said.

Chapter 28

We neared Parkway Center Mall, our rendezvous point for this jaunt up north. I had enjoyed the drive back; we made a few stops and ate dinner at a Red Lobster. Now it was eight o'clock with city lights piercing the darkness.

"We accomplished a lot today, Isis. I'm glad we went. You helped Raven by your intervention."

"I can't believe they didn't call in the authorities, try to do something about her attackers. These crimes will continue—just other names and faces. After the episode with Raven and her friends, Flo was murdered," Isis said.

"I've read a little about black cults, even though this group is much more radical than most. It's amazing, but many of them get away with their crimes and are never punished even if arrested. Evidence disappears. Witnesses refuse to testify. I honestly believe that fear of their dark powers may be at the root of this."

"Or fear they'll strike again. They flaunt the rules of society, don't seem to have any morals. Many of their acts are cruel and malicious."

"So where do we go from here? How do we handle this information Raven has given us? To tell you the truth, I'm a little afraid of getting too close to this group myself. I think calling them evil is putting it mildly."

"Contacting the police is out, per Raven's request, but that is too bad. I would never go against her wishes. The only thing Raven and Flo had in common was their mode of contact—*Pittsburgh Life*. Maybe we should look at a few copies and go from there."

I shivered violently. "Yes, maybe we could call the cult and get inducted into their group."

"We can both work on this project and report back to each other in a few days. I think I see your car."

My battered Escort waited faithfully in the parking lot. In spite of our stops, I felt stiff from riding in the car. I waved as Isis pulled out and I admired the many bumper stickers that adorned her car. One proclaimed that "Vegetarians taste better", another purple and silver glitzy one said "Isis, Isis."

The night was clear and mellow and the drive home whizzed by. My mind continued to turn over the information about the cult from the north, like I worked some puzzle that could be solved if I could only find the right piece.

You black magicians give us witches an extremely bad name. People hear bits and pieces of information and lump us in with the evil people. We're not evil; we seek the light and work for the highest good of all concerned. We never manipulate or harm another.

Then I began to wonder about Raven's description of the leader and his woman. The description was vague, but it could have been

Hank and the diner woman. After all, Hank and she had been right up there near the scene of the crime.

I shook my head. It just didn't make sense. Of course, you never really know another person completely, but I'd known Hank for several years and a murderous cult really didn't fit into my description of him. Maybe the woman had gotten him into it. No, it just didn't fit.

I pulled into my driveway, leaving the Escort outside. I could see Tony next door making trips between his house and his car. His activity caught my interest.

"You going somewhere, Tony?"

"Oh, hi, Stephanie. I'm headed up north. My brother has a little camping place near the state forest. He's going to meet me there."

"Kind of early to be going up there, isn't it?" In the darkness I couldn't make out what he'd packed.

"We're doing some work around the place—clear a few trees that are down, look over the place. It's a beautiful spot on the Clarion River."

"Are you going up tonight?" I asked, knowing the length of the trip since we'd just gone up and back.

"I don't like to travel at night that much. I'll take off in the morning. You certainly have a lot of questions, Steph. Are you sure you aren't some kind of private detective?"

I smiled and my face felt stiff.

“Hey, I was just kidding,” Tony said when I didn’t answer. “You know you’re my very favorite next door neighbor, except maybe for Ginger and the boys.”

Ginger, a single mother with two small sons, lived on the other side of Tony. In spite of myself and my weary condition, I laughed.

“All right, I can tell when I’m not wanted. You go ahead and go up north and take Ginger and the boys with you and try not to get eaten by bears.”

“You ever go up there, Stephanie?” he asked.

I was glad for the darkness that hid my startled expression. I stretched and reasoned that this was a normal question.

“I’ve been up there a few times. It’s beautiful country. I get a feeling of peace in the forest. I can see why you’re going there.”

“Ah well, maybe some time you can come up with me. You’d be good company, Steph.”

I thanked him and went in through our front door. My little house felt especially inviting tonight. I heard Tricksie calling to me as she appeared from our bedroom, looking rumpled and sleepy.

“Did you sleep all day, girl?” I asked as I thoroughly patted her soft fur. She nobly received my display of deep affection.

My thoughts were a tangle of ideas, scenes, and hopes. What was going on, after all? Who was I? Was I the waitress who took pride in her work, or was I someone I didn’t even know?

Tricksie pushed against me, rubbing me, reassuring me that simple explanations were often the best.

* * *

Two mornings later, my answering machine announced "three," the number bright red, and I knew what all the saved messages were this morning.

They were from Alex.

I saved his messages, but hadn't returned them yet. The one last night had been compelling. "Stephanie, this is Alex, your number one admirer. I'd like to spend an evening with you, wine and dine you. I miss holding you in my arms. Please give me a call. My cell phone misses you, too."

I listened to all his messages again, then sat on the bed and reached for the cordless phone. For some strange reason, I couldn't quite reach it.

No, my feelings have changed. Go home to Alice, Alex. Go home to your sweet little roommate, wife, whatever she is, and leave me alone. I want more than exciting sex. I want...

I started crying now, and Tricksie rubbed against me. I wanted to call Alex, but I didn't, and for certain I knew I shouldn't.

Alex was a dead end for sure.

I'd always managed to find the dead end boys as far as relationships were concerned. Alex was no exception to the rule. Maybe if nothing else was in sight I might continue with him like I usually did, sometimes for years.

But now there was Hank. Or was there?

I felt like crying harder, so instead I blew my nose. I remembered the sight of Hank and the woman up at Apple Grove. He'd been coming into the diner regularly now, like always, but I shied away from him because of the woman. And because I didn't understand what he wanted from me or what he had to offer.

I sighed and Tricksie purred louder and I knew it would be all right.

Somehow.

"I'm not calling Alex back. I can't seem to make myself do it, so I give up. If he comes into the diner, I'll just play it by ear," I told Tricksie. She nodded her head imperceptibly, and I knew my decision was sound. Tricksie approved.

"The other thing I'll do is stop avoiding Hank. He's been good to me over the years, and I need to give him a chance. Maybe he'll explain that incident in Apple Grove," I said, the pit of my stomach sinking in spite of my good intentions.

"Or maybe not," I mumbled.

I erased the phone messages, and somehow the red zero didn't look any better than the red three.

I decided to think about all this tomorrow.

* * *

Hank strolled into the diner about five o'clock, looking manly and gorgeous and I caught my breath. I missed being with him.

Unfortunately, the rush had begun early, and Hank had come later than usual, so my resolution to spend time with him had evaporated like the steam in Ruthie's kitchen. Fate must have been against us getting together again.

"You look like you're busy tonight, Stephanie. I'd hoped to talk with you," Hank said from his stool at the counter. The stools beside him were all full, so there wasn't much chance I'd sit with him, even for a minute.

"I don't know where they all come from. There aren't any buses in the parking lot, are there?" I said from behind the counter. Rosemary bustled behind me to cut pie for her customers.

"No buses, I just noticed your Escort."

"Hank," I said suddenly, oblivious to the crowd, noise, and hustle, "I miss being with you. I miss talking to you. I'd like things to get better."

"Me, too, Steph," he said quickly. "I'm not sure what's gone wrong. I'll make it right, whatever it is."

A customer waved at me, and I realized whatever it was we had to say to each other couldn't be here or now.

"Someone wants me over there. Let me take your order. It's nuts in here tonight."

He calmly ordered the special—pork chops and wild rice with green beans and coffee. "I'd like one more thing," he said when I'd already started to go.

"Coconut cream pie later?"

"Pick you up after work. Maybe we can talk a little bit."

I wrote it on my pad and looked up at him. “Got your order, mister. Ruthie’s aims to please its customers. See you a little after eleven, then.”

I felt happier that I had in weeks and all that night, as busy as we were, I kept looking at my watch, watching the hour hand creep toward eleven.

Chapter 29

"I'm a mess," I told Hank when he returned and all the hubbub had died down.

And I was a mess—not only on the inside with my customary emotional turmoil—but on the outside, too. My lemon blouse was stained with catsup and grease, and I'd spilled cold coffee on my pants. My hair stuck out every which way, my face felt greasy, my legs ached, and my fingernails looked ragged.

"You look fine," he said, looking me up and down. "Actually, better than fine."

"Maybe I should go home and change," I said, knowing if I went home I'd crash on the sofa.

"If you want to, of course you can. But I've seen you more messed up than that over the years. I like you however you look, Stephanie."

"I'll just go straighten my hair, then we can figure out what we're doing. Thanks for coming back," I said with a genuine smile.

"At your service, lady." He bowed and I felt properly courted.

When I returned, face replenished and hair under control, my purse over one shoulder, I felt ready for the prom.

Well, almost ready.

"Want to come to my place?" Hank asked as we moved through the diner doors.

I only hesitated a second. "It's not far away from here, is it?"

"That's the only difficulty I've had to overcome all these years. It takes me about an hour and a half to get here, but you're worth it." His serious gaze tugged at my heart. I stared at him, but I thought I saw his mouth twitch.

"I don't think so," I said. "You once told me you live on the way to Weirton, West Virginia."

"I do. It'll take us twenty minutes to get there. I just wanted to impress you."

As we chattered, I thought I saw the black Cadillac sport utility vehicle in the back part of the lot. It was dark back there, and it could have been someone else's, not Alex's.

Before I got in Hank's Bronco, I remembered the lateness of the hour and my past experience with Alex. "Maybe I should drive and follow you in my car. Then you won't have to drive me home."

He agreed, though he acted like he wanted me beside him.

The trip was short and uneventful, Hank easy to follow. He drove off a side road that looped around revealing dark wooden homes with skylights. His was no exception; he pulled into the driveway of a dark wooden ranch with long windows, skylights, and expert landscaping. The street lights illuminated the modern-looking architecture.

"This is really nice," I said soberly. This place spoke of the establishment. I could make out the bright yellow of several blooming forsythia bushes, and an azalea in bud. We'd been having mild weather, even some days in the seventies. Several rhododendron bushes also decorated the front of the house, and would bloom later in the season.

"I'm glad you like it," he said from inside the two-car garage where he'd pulled his vehicle. The garage was clean and orderly with a work bench and metal shelving, items neatly stored.

"Come on in," he said, opening a door into the house. He turned on lights as we walked through an orderly kitchen with hanging green plants, a hallway, and then into a large living room.

Light colors softened the inside of the house, in contrast to its dark, forest-like exterior. The living room carpet lay light yellow and soft plush to my feet, the sofa a medium green and comfortable-looking, the armchairs flowered brocade. The overall impression was expensive and well done.

A comforting noise caught my ear, and in one corner of the room water cascaded down around a statue of an Oriental woman.

"Is that Kwan Yin?" I asked in amazement, gazing at my favorite Chinese goddess.

"None other. Do you like her? I figured I could use a little warmth and compassion in my life."

"She's beautiful. I've always been drawn to her—sort of an earth mother goddess spreading nurturing and love."

"Sit down, Stephanie. Want some music?" he said, pointing to an elaborate stereo system.

I nodded, unsure of myself, and he pushed buttons until relaxing melodies issued from the speakers. Classical music poured out, soothing and intelligent.

"Would you like something to drink? I have beer, wine, water, Pepsi, maybe a wine cooler."

I couldn't help but smile at this scenario. "So the customer is waiting on the waitress? A wine cooler would be fine."

He left for just a few minutes, but I panned the room, drinking in its beauty. This space spoke of peace and grace, and felt like a place of healing, especially when overseen by Kwan Yin. I felt instantly at home here, just as I had with Hank.

He returned with a lemon-lime wine cooler and clear wine glass for me, a beer in a mug for himself, and then settled beside me on the couch. For a few minutes we listened to the fountain as Kwan Yin bestowed her blessings upon us. No one had anything to say.

"I didn't expect this to be easy," I finally said.

"Talking about emotional matters and personal stuff has never been my strong point. I can lecture before students for hours, and talk with all sorts of people on diverse subjects, but feelings somehow stymie me."

I patted his hand. "We'll get it all sorted out, Hank. I think everyone has good intentions."

"What's gone wrong, Steph? I sense a distancing in you. I don't think it was coming from me. We were doing pretty well, then I went on my trip, and when I came back you wouldn't come near me or talk much to me. Is it just because I went away?"

In my agitation, wine cooler spilled down the front of my shirt, which added nicely to the catsup stains. Hank handed me a napkin, and I marveled at how easily he slipped into the serving role.

"I didn't want to bring this up, Hank, because I guess it's none of my business. I'm not sure how to approach this, either. Let me just ask you what type of a relationship you're looking for—something with commitment or a no-questions-asked arrangement?"

He leaned back on the couch beside me and held his chin in one hand. "Somehow this is more intense than what I expected," he said.

"I'm an intense woman and this is an intense situation."

"If I understand your questions correctly, even though we've barely operated outside the diner at this point, you can be sure that my feelings have always included loyalty to you. I guess commitment might depend on you."

I fidgeted on the sofa.

"Are you seeing another woman?" I finally asked.

"Is that what this is all about? Where have you gotten these ideas? I have a few friends who are women, but they're only friends. Have you ever seen me with another woman?" He sounded mystified.

"Yes, I have."

"You have?" Hank's voice rose as he rose a few inches off the couch.

"I didn't want to act possessive or browbeat you. My friend Deborah and I went on a little trip up to the mountains. We drove up to Apple Grove and saw you in the diner there with some dark-haired woman. She seemed quite taken with you."

"You were in Apple Grove? Stephanie, what were you doing in Apple Grove?"

We stared at each other a full five seconds before I started laughing. Then we were both laughing and he reached over and hugged me to him, a long, lingering hug. My body melted at his touch, and I trusted him; he was my man. Everything would fall into place.

"All right," Hank said when we'd separated to our respective spots on the couch, "I obviously want to make this right. I can see why you would think poorly of me. She's a business contact of mine."

"Business contact? I thought you were on a vacation taking care of family business. Did you take her on vacation?" My voice reached an accusatory peak, much to my disappointment. I hated playing the jealous female.

"I wasn't on vacation. I was working, but I don't like to divulge my second job. Secrecy seems to suit the profession."

"What is your second job?"

"Do I have to tell you?" He shifted on the couch.

"No, not at all." I smiled sweetly at him as I got up. "I'll just be on my way. Thanks for everything."

"Sit down, girl. I do private investigating work for companies and individuals—wherever I can get a referral, as long as I find the case appealing. I worked in the area previously for families whose children had fallen into a cult. One of them gave me the okay to investigate the Flo Pohaski burning because it seemed related. We've had so few leads into this group that I've had to grab onto anything."

"So who was your contact?" I tried to ask casually, but my hands gripped the sofa arm. I hoped I wouldn't leave marks.

"Jeanie works independently, too. She's been investigating for a separate set of parents, so we collaborate on the information whenever possible."

"She was getting into collaborating, as I recall. She was gazing adoringly into your eyes as she touched you fondly."

"Jeanie's got a thing for me."

"I noticed."

"But did you see me gazing adoringly at her mouth—which never shuts—or touching her anywhere or showing much interest at all?"

I frowned as I concentrated.

"No, you weren't returning her flirtation. That didn't occur to me."

"I rest my case. I am not guilty of running up to Apple Grove for a rendezvous with some noisy woman I'm not even attracted to.

"Now, the question that burns in my brain, which I can hardly wait for you to answer is: What were you and your friend doing in Apple Grove? It's not a popular vacation spot. It's barely on the map.

"What exactly was your connection with Flo Pohaski?"

Chapter 30

"Have you found the cult? Have you found the leaders of the group?" I asked quietly.

"Very little information. All my leads dry up like a creek in August. Every time I think I'm getting somewhere, a witness refuses to talk. I've seen fuzzy pictures of the high priest and priestess, but we don't even have names."

"Flo Pohaski belonged to the Women's Healing Circle in Pittsburgh. Deborah helped found the group seven years ago. I joined last summer. Have you heard of us?"

"You're a group of women who call themselves witches, a harmless group, observing rituals and living close to the earth. White witches."

"I couldn't have stated it better myself," I said in astonishment, impressed with his knowledge. "Flo belonged to our group, but she had a run-in with Isis—better known as Deborah—and she quit our group. We were just in the process of trying to locate Flo when she hit the news."

"Unfinished business?"

"That's it. I think Isis felt guilty about the situation because Flo got mad at us and joined this other group. So when we learned of her unusual death, Isis wanted to find out who did it."

"And you, Stephanie? Do you want to find out who did it?"

I thought a minute. "I guess it's not that important to me. I only knew her a few months after all. But that explains why we were at Apple Grove. We were investigating Flo's murder."

"So we're both investigators. And you thought I was involved with Jeanie, so that's why you backed out on me."

"I'm pretty jumpy," I said, thinking about the rest—how I'd gotten involved with Alex, fearing the worst about Hank. Did I really have any good reason to expect Hank's loyalty?

"Does that about cover it? Are we squared away now?" he asked.

"I feel a lot better now. I realize how a misunderstanding can create problems where none exist. I'm glad you were willing to talk about this. Maybe you can tell me something I've wanted to know."

"Of course." He smiled in an eager and open way.

"Were you able to trace the *Pittsburgh Life* ad that the cult ran? That was the only lead we could find and the only thing Flo and Raven had in common."

"Who's Raven?"

"She's a teenager who got involved with the black magic people. She told Deborah and me her story, but she swore us to secrecy. Both Flo and Raven got involved through this newspaper ad."

"One of my clients did, too. I did pursue that lead, but it got me nowhere. It led to a post office box that was no longer functioning. The ad itself was no longer in the paper as of four or five months ago. It was evidently a short-term mechanism.

"I'm not sure how these people operate, where they get their converts. Teenagers are often involved because they're looking for a different way of life; they're more open. But I do know one thing."

"What's that, Hank?"

"I've never seen a more demented, sicko group of people. They're evil." I felt his sincerity, and it struck a chord in me, too.

"I haven't seen much of them, but it looks that way to me, too. Our Flo could be very annoying and petty, but she never deserved such vicious treatment from whoever they were."

"That's the nature of these people, whatever their motivation."

Shortly afterward I excused myself, reluctant to leave Hank's beautiful surroundings, wanting to be with Hank, but still afraid to trust.

I drove home deep in thought. Once, I looked up and imagined I saw a black sport utility vehicle behind me in the distance. Part of my mind remained with Alex, and I couldn't help noticing that I missed him. Now that I'd decided to stop seeing him, he was more attractive than ever.

You have demons in you, woman. I smiled to myself and told the demons to go far, far away.

* * *

I'm not a snoop. I'm really not. This business with Flo and Isis changed me somewhat so that I looked at things differently now. I'd become suspicious and edgy. And information had become essential.

So that when Tony left his garage door open this morning, I began to wonder if there weren't any clues over there. After all, he'd admitted to taking a trip up north to the mountains. I felt the answer to this Flo puzzle lay nearby. It could be someone I knew.

Actually, I saw Tony driving off in his car. I was standing at my front window eating a bagel. I dropped the bagel back onto its dish and waited for Tony to drive out of sight.

"I've got to go over there, Tricksie. Maybe there's something Tony is concealing. I have to be quick about it, though."

I knew Tricksie would show an interest in my buttered bagel, but I left it behind to keep my senses acute and clear.

I glanced in the direction Tony had gone, my heart thumping. The fact that he'd left the garage door open increased the probability that he'd be coming right back.

I eased my way into the garage and saw shelving filled haphazardly with items: cans of paint, newspapers, cleaners, and lubricating sprays. A bicycle leaned in one corner, a bicycle pump, and some boots.

All in all, everything looked quite ordinary, not one diabolical ritual item in the lot. Yet I couldn't leave yet; a ladder beckoned to me. At the rear of the garage I could see the opening into the rafters with the blonde wood ladder pulled down—access to the attic.

I felt my heart thumping harder as I climbed the steps, for I knew I'd passed the point of no return. I couldn't get out of this if he came back.

I reached the attic area and looked around at a huge assortment of articles. Tony must have squirreled away everything he'd bought in the past twenty years. A piece of wood caught my eye, so I carefully stepped through the treasures to gaze behind large boxes. I wiggled boxes around until I could clearly see the wood item.

Carefully positioned on its side rested a large wooden cross.

I didn't get to look at it carefully because I heard a car motor approaching, and I scrambled down the ladder. I turned to look at Tony, who'd parked outside the garage. His expression ranged somewhere between surprised and puzzled.

"Hi," he said. "I just ran to the post office, so I didn't bother closing the garage door. Is there something I can help you with?"

I hesitated, nearly telling him the truth. I was horrified he'd caught me in his garage attic. My gentle neighbor didn't deserve this kind of treatment.

"Have you seen Tricksie? I think she got out. I haven't been able to find her," I said. I could feel my knees quivering.

"Gosh Steph, you scared me. So you were just looking for your cat. I wasn't sure what to make of you in here. Was she up there?" He motioned to the ladder.

"I don't think so. I called her, but I didn't hear anything. Cats can hide away in the most unusual places." I eased out of the garage, glancing over at my house. Tricksie calmly sat in the front window licking my bagel. At any moment my cover would be blown.

Tony stood with his back to my house. I held my breath and tried to imagine him getting into his car and driving into the garage without looking around.

"I do apologize. I should have waited till you got back home to look for Tricksie. I get so anxious when I can't find her."

"That's all right. I'll leave the ladder down in case she's up there. She's probably out in the woods terrorizing the little furry creatures."

"So sorry, Tony."

"Quite all right. I trust you, after all, dear neighbor lady."

But do I trust you, I wondered? What's that cross doing in your attic, I wanted to ask? All the while I held in my mind the picture of Tony wearing blinders, driving into his garage and shutting the door.

I stood and waved as he did just that, and sighed from the bottom of my toes in relief as the garage door shuddered into place. I turned, and Tricksie stared at me from her perch in our living room window. She stood on her back legs and pawed at the glass, one of her habits that made her especially conspicuous at this moment.

I raced home, then decided to cover my tracks a bit more. I ran back over and rang Tony's doorbell, embracing Tricksie to my chest.

"Say, you found the old girl," he said cheerfully.

"You'll never guess where she was," I said as Tricksie began to wiggle.

"The woods."

"In my house. She was prancing around when I got back from your place. Must have been hiding in the house somewhere. And I wasn't even taking her to the vet. Guess we'd better go. Thanks again, Tony," I said as Tricksie's movements became more violent.

I got back to the front door just in time to drop her inside. She plunked loudly as she hit the rug, and her beige fur belly swung back and forth as she switched her tail in vexation.

"Now, Trickster, it's your job to cover for me. After all, I worry about your safety continuously, and it's a small price to pay for cat chow and all those cat toys."

Tricksie marched over and attacked her cardboard scratching tray and I tried to grasp the importance of my discovery in Tony's attic.

Whatever use could he have for a large, wooden cross?

What was it doing in his attic?

Chapter 31

I found the Shadyside Center for the Arts and parked the Escort up the hill from it. Dusk rapidly approached, so I hustled across the cobblestones, past the picturesque cottage-looking building to the park, Mellon Park.

The grass lay green and expansive, especially for here in the city, and the trees rose tall and majestic. I could hear city traffic over the crest of the hill, but I seemed far removed from it here. It felt like I'd entered an English manor estate. All it lacked were the peacocks patrolling the grounds.

A huge tree dead ahead with widespread branches sheltered our group. Several of the women waved to me, and I waved back, grateful to locate them so easily. Seven sat around the circle, and they rearranged themselves to make a spot for me.

I'd worn a black cloak thrown over a simple long dress with small lavender flowers and green leaves. For late March, it was unseasonable warm. The sunny day had left the ground warm beneath the comforter I'd brought.

"Stephanie, I just announced that this is the Women's Healing Circle. We have two guests tonight, but it was almost three," Isis said. The ladies laughed, and I waited for the punch line.

"Barry Goodman tried to join us, so I had to tell him this is for women only. Do you think that's fair?"

I laughed. "He could have at least disguised himself, worn a scarf on his head. We have to have our standards, Isis."

I saw her smile, though she looked tired tonight.

"Tonight our intention for the full moon ritual is manifesting abundance in our lives. We will call upon the Hindu Goddess Lakshmi. I hope you've all brought symbols of the abundance you want to bring into your life. You can place those items on the altar to bless them."

I looked at the shiny gold and white cloth arranged at the center of our circle lit by candles. White tea lights circled us, laid out about every foot, shining happily in the approaching darkness.

I fingered the rose quartz heart I held. It felt warm from my grasping of it, and it fit neatly into one hand. I placed it on the altar, imparting my intention to it.

Please, Goddess Lakshmi, please hear my prayer. Please bring me abundance in love, a special love with a special man.

I shivered as I placed it near a lavender pillar candle. It had been a long time since I had asked for love. I'd given up on it with my teenage dreams. This heart of stone symbolized my heart of stone, but it was pink, the color of divine love, and rose quartz was claimed to be a healer of hearts.

I sat back and caught the magic. These rituals were infinitely satisfying to me, especially those held outdoors. Even the ones held at Friend's Meeting House in an upstairs room felt powerful, with our altar on the floor, a cloth laid out with candles blazing.

But tonight in the growing darkness below this wise old tree with these gentle women, I felt alive and full of purpose. I looked up and beheld the moon for the first time tonight. The moon reigned large and golden, filling the night sky, but wouldn't be full for a few days yet. Isis wouldn't be available then, so we held our ritual tonight. Even witches compromise at times.

Our ritual flowed easily this evening. We called on the four directions, turning as we called forth the powers of the north, east, south, and west. We sang songs of empowerment, and Isis invoked Lakshmi to bring us abundance. Later on, we wrote on slips of paper what kind of abundance we wanted to manifest in our lives.

I hesitated briefly, and then committed my thoughts to paper: Please Goddess, send a man who will love me. And please let me love him back. Abundance in love.

We committed our papers to Lakshmi, said a blessing again, made a circle within our circle, and closed our ritual. Afterward, we talked for several minutes, laughing as we tried to retrieve our belongings in the semi-darkness.

"Don't blow out the candles until we've gotten everything," Sara said.

We strolled across the expanse of lawn, admiring the gorgeous moon lighting our pathway. I broke away from the group, striding up the sidewalk. I remembered I hadn't told Isis about Tony and the cross. I was tired and wanted to be home, so I shook my head and continued to the car. I'd handle that one later.

I sensed someone behind me as I inserted the car key. I knew who it was.

"Stephanie," I heard, and then felt a hand on my shoulder.

I jumped anyway, leaving the keys dangling in the car door.

"Alex, you scared me. I thought I was being mugged. I almost jammed my elbow into you." I decided to be dramatic.

He stood tall beside me, wearing a black turtleneck and slacks. "At least, then, I'd know you still cared. Why haven't you returned my phone calls?"

"I want a man of my own. When I first got involved with you, I didn't know about Alice. I'm just an on-the-side affair. If I don't get top billing, I don't play the show."

"I didn't know you felt that way. I thought we had something good going, some genuine, pure animal lust. You ought not to thumb your nose at primal sex. Wasn't it good for you?"

"There's more to a relationship than sex. I'm trying to retrain myself so that I can receive a more in-depth and fulfilling type of arrangement."

"We belong together." He'd put his hand on my arm and his touch felt comforting. I could feel my resolve fading away.

"I need to go home right now. I appreciate that you went to all this trouble to see me. We'll talk again later." With a stab of remorse, I kissed him tenderly, the sparks lighting up the night air, and then I jumped into the Escort.

On the ride home, the lights of the city seemed especially bright. I'd expected Alex to reenter my life, but not this way. He must have followed me and maybe had been doing so for a while. His method of operation seemed creepy, and I felt my privacy had been invaded.

Was Alex the answer to my prayer to Lakshmi?

You don't work that fast, do you, Goddess? Besides, Alex doesn't seem to be the answer to anyone's prayer, not even his roommate Alice's.

* * *

I dreamed that night, the images vivid and colorful. I awoke in a sweat, gasping for air, but Tricksie took care of me until I was calm again.

I'd seen Hank up on a hill, his hands tied behind him around a tree. He kept calling my name, searching for me, but he was frozen and unable to move. His face and cries revealed his acute anxiety.

Alex was everywhere. Every time I looked in a new spot, he appeared there, beckoning to me. He looked sad, anxious like Hank, but in a different way.

"Come home to me. We have always belonged together. I've waited so long to be with you." Alex held out his arms to me.

In the distance, I could hear the crackling of flames, I could see the fire rising high into the sky.

In the dream, Alex's request seemed reasonable, so that I went to him and he held me firmly, almost savagely, in his arms. "Don't ever go away again. We will have a wonderful life together. We'll go to the finest restaurants, travel to Europe or wherever else you want to go. We'll live like royalty."

As he held me, I could hear Hank's voice drifting down from far away. He called to me, saying, "Stephanie, I'm coming. Wait right there. I'm coming. Don't be afraid."

Hank's voice woke me up, as if I'd been dreaming within my dream. I felt panic and wondered if Hank would ever come. So that when I woke up, Hank was on my mind. I felt an overwhelming urge to run to him, to be him in his house.

"Tricksie," I said as I wiped sweat off with the sheet. "I want to be with Hank more than ever, but it never seems to work out. Tell me what I should do, girl."

"Mah," she said, her rusty owl eyes somber. "Mah."

Chapter 32

The sun shone strongly on Easter Sunday, promising a brilliant spring. The daffodils and narcissuses at Tony's danced in the breeze and I could see the azalea bushes in front of our green house budded and ready to burst into pink and red display. What a beautiful, full-of-promise day.

Yet I felt restless and discontent. I hadn't seen Hank in the past few days, which hadn't bothered me before. That was his pattern—he'd come in every day for weeks, then disappear for days or nearly a week. I shouldn't have felt any concern, yet my surprise meeting with Alex had unsettled me. I looked for him now behind every tree, every parked car, even around my house. I feared he'd turn up again, yet part of me missed him, even felt a longing for him.

That's why I needed Hank now, why his absence mattered more than normal. Hank was solid and real—he centered me—and I needed him to pull me back now from the abyss beyond which Alex dwelled.

Three times this morning I'd picked up the phone to call Hank, but each time I failed to make the connection. I just couldn't do it. I didn't know what was wrong with me, but I did know I wanted Hank now.

So I fervently wished he'd show up at the diner or call me. As I got ready for work, I wished even harder, so that when I got to work and didn't see his Bronco, I was disappointed. This was earlier than he usually came in, I conceded.

As the evening wore on, I nearly forgot about missing Hank. My favorite diners came in, and the mood turned quite jovial. The pace was steady, but not too busy. This was waitressing at its best. I was grateful Ruthie stayed open on Easter.

Regardless, when Hank strode in about seven p.m., I felt a rush of relief and joy. He looked handsome in his red plaid shirt and black corduroy pants as he advanced to the counter and plunked onto a stool.

"I'm glad to see you, Hank. I've missed you," I said as I poured him a cup of coffee. I brushed against his arm and felt happy.

"That's what I like, a proper greeting. And I'm even later than my usual arrival time. I missed you, too. I always miss you when I don't come in."

He ordered dinner, eating meditatively as I went about my work. The dinner crowd had thinned down considerable so that by the time he was ready for dessert, I could park myself on the stool next to him

"Where's your pie?" he asked as I presented him with cherry pie a la mode.

I fingered the glass of ginger ale I'd poured myself.

"My stomach's been a little queasy lately. I don't need the calories, anyway." It was true—since Alex had startled me in the dark, my appetite had been off. My own diagnosis was tension creating gastrointestinal unrest. Whatever it was, food didn't always look appealing to me these days.

"Have you been away? Any progress on the cult story?" I asked him.

"I've just been doing some work for school, no investigating lately. Believe it or not, I've got to do my primary job. It's top priority."

"But the other is more interesting?"

"In some ways, yes, fascinating. But this cult has been so elusive, I have to say it's been interesting, but totally frustrating. I've just about resigned myself to the fact that I'll never get enough information to get this group stopped.

"You know," he said and turned to me, "I don't even care if they're caught and punished. My main concern is that they be stopped. I want the acts of cruelty to stop. I want them out of business. Permanently."

I shivered, feeling the strength of his convictions. "You're absolutely right. From what I've learned, their group needs obliterated, which would mean getting to those at the top—the High Priest and Priestess. I get the feeling if you can get rid of them, the cult would crumble away."

"That's astute of you, Steph. I think you're right. Without the leaders, these atrocities wouldn't be happening."

"What do you know about these leaders?"

"Very little. Like I said, I've seen pictures of the High Priest and Priestess taken at a distance. I've talked to some of their followers, but they've covered their tracks efficiently. There's only one thing those two do better than maiming and torturing the innocent."

"What's that?"

"Keeping themselves anonymous. It's as if they don't exist. They evaporate into the atmosphere after each deranged ritual."

"You know, there's only one person I dread more than this diabolical couple," I said, restraining a smile.

"Who might that be?" He paused from eating to look me squarely in the eyes.

"Jeanie the investigator, the one I saw you with in Apple Grove."

"Oh, I know who you mean. Once again, your judgment is impeccable. I always head the other way if I can when she's around. Those jaws work endlessly, and I've had to listen to more boring trivia to get to the few bits of information I really need.

"She's like a fly in my oatmeal."

I smiled and sipped at my ginger ale. Rosemary made funny faces at me and pointed somewhere behind where we sat.

I turned around as Alex came even with me. He modeled a black business suit cut to show off his slender figure, a blue shirt, and black and silver tie.

"Stephanie," he said in his most charming voice, "I'd like to see you. I know you're working now, but I can always come back later."

"This isn't a good time, Alex," I said, unsure how to handle the situation with Hank beside me. "Maybe next week. I haven't been feeling well lately."

Neither man appeared to notice the other. I realized this might alter things between Hank and me. I couldn't exactly lie about Alex. At best, I hoped Hank might not ask any questions.

"You'll be sorry when I'm gone," Alex said, his face hardening. He turned on one heel of his expensive Italian loafers, and breezed out.

Hank threw down some bills and stood up just after Alex had gone.

"I have some questions for you, but just now I'm on a job. I'll see you later."

I grabbed his shirt sleeve.

"What is it, Hank?"

"I just had a close encounter with the cult leader. Got to follow him. Bye."

He kissed my cheek and disappeared into the night.

I was left with such a mixture of strong emotions I didn't know whether to cry, scream, or run laps around the diner. I'd become an instant mess. The urge to follow both men had come and gone.

I knew I had to finish my shift, even if my personal life had just crashed and was burning.

What was Hank thinking about me and Alex, I wondered? Would I have to confess my sexual relationship with him?

Was Alex really the cult leader? Had I been consorting with the enemy?

If Alex was such a bad guy, why did I have feelings for him? Why had I even met him in K-Mart in the first place?

My stomach performed major flip flops by now and my hands sweated. I even dropped a plate, which shattered on the floor.

Rosemary came over as I picked up the pieces.

"Why don't you go in the back and relax?" she said, rubbing my back. "We're not busy now, anyway."

"You're always so kind, Rose. Thank you for your help. I'd better just work. I can't sit still right now. I'm too agitated."

"Just so you're all right," she said, concern etched into her features.

"I'll tell you what. One more broken dish or glass and I'll knock it off. I'll feel better if I stay around till my shift's over."

How could I leave when the drama continued out there somewhere? Waiting here at Ruthie's was pure torture, but all I could do.

An hour later, my prayers were answered. Hank reentered the diner and sank into a booth at the side. He looked collected, but when I went over to pour him coffee, I noticed a scowl about his features. When he looked up to greet me, he smiled and I wondered if I'd imagined his distress.

"Wild goose chase," he said as he sipped at the coffee. "Do you have a minute?"

I felt relief that Alex had gotten away, but my throat and chest tightened when I anticipated a conversation with Hank. I didn't want to talk about Alex. That was off limits; besides, I didn't think Hank would understand my affair with Alex that had been ignited by the scene between him and Jeanie.

"Sure, Hank, in a few minutes. Let me check on my customers first."

I stalled as long as I could, even went in the back room and hung out a few minutes and talked to Rosemary as she smoked a cigarette.

"He's going to know you're avoiding him," she said as she stubbed out the butt.

"I know. I'm going out there right now. To face the music."

"More like the male ego," Rosemary said.

"To be honest, in the past my female ego hasn't operated at full capacity, either."

Rosemary hugged me quickly. "Some couplings were meant to be. My husband and I are like that. And you and Hank are like that. I knew a long time before either one of you showed an interest in the other."

I gave a Mona Lisa smile, and warm-hearted Rosemary rushed in once again to console me.

"Trust it, Stephanie. For heaven's sake, just trust it."

Chapter 33

I straightened my hair and put on lipstick before sauntering back out to the dining room. Curiosity seized me; I wondered how the chase after Alex had gone.

"Stephanie, I get the feeling you'd rather not talk to me about this man. I promise I'll make it as painless as possible," Hank said, looking up from the booth seat. I slid into the other side. The dining room had just about cleared out, so I felt relaxed about taking time off.

"What happened? Where did Alex go?"

"I saw him get into the black Cadillac vehicle and followed him, thinking he hadn't seen me. He got on 79 north and shot right up the interstate. I stayed back as far as I could.

"I thought I saw him get off the Cranberry exit. A bunch of cars and trucks exited together. By the time I got off and through the traffic, I'd lost him. He could have pulled in anywhere. I'd counted on him being unaware of me, but I must have been wrong.

"He slipped away from me so easily," Hank said.

"What would you have done if you'd successfully followed him?" I asked.

"I'm not totally unsuccessful. I have his license plate number. I should be able to trace his identity. I've never gotten this close before, Stephanie. I also wanted to follow him home, see the dwelling, maybe question the neighbors later. But at least I have something."

"You weren't going to confront him?"

"I'd like to. I'd like to get the monster, but that's why I'm an investigator and not a law enforcer. I just dig up the info and try to get these guys nailed."

Something kept fluttering at the back of my mind like a small butterfly. Something was amiss, a piece missing from this puzzle. My emotional attachments blinded me. At last, my mind cleared.

"Earlier this evening you said you'd only seen pictures of the leaders of this cult taken from a distance. How can you be sure Alex is the High Priest?"

Hank hesitated. "I just knew. As soon as I laid eyes on him, I got strong feelings. Hunches have served me well in this work."

"But you could be wrong. You could have the wrong man." I wanted to believe my own words.

Hank drank coffee for a few minutes, giving me a meditative stare. "I suppose you're right. I could be wrong. Maybe I'm jumping to all the wrong conclusions, but my batting average is pretty good. I'm rarely wrong when I get a strong hunch."

We sat in companionable silence for a few minutes so that I forgot to be fearful of our conversation. Just as I relaxed completely, Hank focused on my worst fears.

"Tell me, who is this Alex?"

My relaxation came to my rescue, for the words flowed easily from me. "We met in K-Mart. We literally ran into each other because he was talking on his cell phone. He likes to take me out to eat, and he traced me here to the diner. In fact, you two nearly ran into each other once before.

"He's a developer—of malls, he said. I know very little about him. We both feel like we've known each other in a past lifetime. He lives with a woman on the east side of town."

Hank's eyes widened. "Have you gone there?"

"To their apartment?" I couldn't quite comprehend his question. When he nodded, I replied, "No, never. Alex and I socialized over here or in town."

"Was there ever a reference to the cult or his position as High Priest?"

"Alex is a guy who goes to malls by day, restaurants and bars by night. Never once did he refer to any religion or cult or deviant ritual. Honestly, you've got the wrong guy. I'm not sure where you're coming from," I said, my voice intensifying so that I knew I was talking too loud, my frayed nerves showing.

"How long have you known him, Steph?"

"Two months. I haven't even been seeing him lately. Honestly, I barely know him."

I could see the wheels turning in Hank's head. I was deathly afraid the next question would be about our sexual status. I jumped up and straightened my apron.

"I hope that will help you, Hank. If I think of anything else, I'll be sure and tell you. I just think Alex is a city dweller who enjoys the company of women. He's a typical man with a typical lust for wealth and power. I don't think he has any unusual depravities."

"I have to ask you one more thing," Hank said, grabbing my hand.

My heart thumped erratically, and I nodded. This was getting entirely too personal.

"If you see him again, can you keep your eyes open for clues, for any signs that might connect him with the cult? Perhaps in your conversation you might gently lead him there and see what happens. You're my only lead, Stephanie." He squeezed my hand and released it.

What a bittersweet moment, for I was caught between two worlds, between two men I loved in very different ways. Hank seemed so steady and earth-bound, yet my heart leaped each time I beheld him.

Alex truly was a mystery and full of the unknown, a creature of the night and of his own desires, a family man of some sort with his lady Alice. Yet the unknown became the known-once-before when we were together, as our feelings coincided. We knew we had been together before; this wasn't the first time our worlds had collided. No matter who or where we had been, some close connection had bound us, even as we had come together once again.

"Anything else you're thinking about?" Hank's eyes showed concern only, no accusations or fear.

"I guess I spaced out a minute there. This is all such a shock. I never expected any of this."

"I'm sorry to ask you these questions, but I do feel strongly about the evil spread by these people. I won't rest until we stop them."

"I'm glad for your work, Hank. Yes, I'll try to get information, but I stopped seeing Alex. Do you want me to get together with him?"

"No, I don't. If for some reason you see him or talk to him, fine. Please don't see him if you don't want to. After all, you would be in danger, too. Do nothing to endanger yourself."

Hank got up to go then, too. We embraced, and I felt his strength. I wanted to go with him, but I had a few more hours on my shift.

"We'll get through this, Steph. When it's all over, you and I can enjoy ourselves properly. I've never met another woman with your intellect, charm, and natural beauty. I've always just wanted to be with you." His green eyes stared into mine now. "It doesn't matter about this Alex guy."

I nodded, my chest and throat too tight to reply.

Suddenly, I just wanted to go home and collapse.

* * *

That night I dreamed of Kwan Yin, but not a statue—a living, breathing Oriental woman wearing a beautiful embroidered red silk sheath dress. Her black hair was piled high on her head, white pearls and gold chains around her neck, and garnet and pearl earrings shining from her ears.

We stood outside amongst ponds where goldfish swam, with delicate lily pads, the flowers purple, yellow, and pink. Willow trees lent charm to the scene, their branches bowing low, as if they were courtly gentlemen paying respect to us.

The sky beamed radiantly at us, a startling blue that reflected in the ponds. Such energy and vitality the sun and sky emitted, and it was all reflected in the face of Kwan Yin. For that was what struck me most about her, her radiant countenance.

Kwan Yin immediately looked at me, and I sensed her energy. Her face and skin glowed, and I wondered at how alive she seemed. Everything about her—her movements, her looks—spoke of vitality and great energy.

"Come with me, my child," she said, sensing my unrest. She led me to a bench in the sun and we sat side by side. I felt for a second that we might be sisters settling down for a chat.

"You must rest your mind, my child. I watch over you. Even though all is confusion, order will someday be apparent." Kwan Yin spoke in well-modulated tones. She looked so young, young enough to be my kid sister, yet her wise words calmed me more than any sedative.

"Can I ask you questions, Kwan Yin?"

"Ask whatever you will. I have come to assure you your hopes and dreams are a high priority. All is going well for you, despite your fears."

I watched the orange fish swim in the pond. Their movements somehow comforted me.

"Is Alex the High Priest of the cult?" I asked.

"You will know very soon. Part of you knows already."

"Am I in danger?"

"Not when I watch over you. You are protected."

"Will Hank and I be together?"

"You see him now, don't you?"

I nodded.

"My protection covers your love relationships, child. You will be protected and guided in these matters."

We walked onto an arched bridge over a pond. I suddenly felt a lifting of my cares and worries. I felt a connection with this goddess who was so compassionate and personable.

When I woke up, it seemed so real. I would never think about Kwan Yin the same after that. Even the smallest statue would trigger a feeling of deepest devotion in me.

Chapter 34

I spied the moon from Ruthie's parking lot and caught my breath. What a glorious, powerful, beautiful moon! It hung low in the sky, huge and orange, and I felt like I could almost touch it. Magic must surely be afoot.

I threw my jacket and purse in the car. The warm evening comforted me; a breeze caressed my neck. A delicious scent filled my senses—hyacinths blooming in front of the diner.

I'd grown weary from my labors, from the emotional turmoil of my life. I slipped behind the wheel of the faithful Escort and steered home this night after my shift. The night was a blur, and I knew I must be tired, getting run down, for I couldn't remember the details of my evening. It was as if part of me was gone, and the me who remained was just going through the motions.

I drove almost home before I noticed the black Cadillac sport utility vehicle in my rear view mirror. I knew who it was, yet I felt nothing—not fear, joy, excitement, nor even dread. I'd not heard from him since the scene in the diner, when he intersected paths with Hank. I needed to talk with him, but I wasn't in any hurry.

I parked in my garage, closing the garage door, not seeing the Cadillac anywhere. Peering through the small garage door windows, I saw nothing—no cars moving, no people out, just lights in the houses across the street and over at Tony's.

I must be imagining all this. I'm finally losing it.

Tricksie greeted me in the house, establishing a feeling of normalcy, rubbing me and soothing me with cat noises.

The doorbell rang.

Both Tricksie and I jumped, and my heart began to thump in my chest. I felt so rattled, I nearly ran into the bedroom and hid. Oddly, there was no car parked in my driveway. I opened the front door cautiously, seeing him through a small opening, hesitating to fling it wide as I had in the past.

"It's just me, Stephanie, for God's sake."

"I'm glad you've come, Alex. Come in."

He swept past me, wearing the black turtleneck and slacks, turning in mid living room. "I'm sorry I haven't gotten back to you sooner, honey. I felt pretty rejected when you didn't want to see me in the diner. You've been rejecting me every chance you get. I nearly gave up on you entirely. I thought we were better friends than this."

He grabbed my hands and held them, gazing softly into my eyes.

"I'm sorry, Alex. I've always loved being with you." Again, I felt the old attraction—whatever bound us together—the excitement and an acute interest in this man.

"I've worried about you at the same time I've been cringing from your rejection. Let's sit down, dear." He paused as we sat near each other on the couch, our legs touching.

"Why would you worry about me?" I asked.

"I know that man who sat beside you at the diner. I know you're connected with him somehow, and he's not a safe person to get close to." He wore a worried look that complemented his words.

"What do you mean?" I felt my face flush.

"His name is Hank Shepherd. He's a master at disguise and telling lies. He's also the leader of a cult of deviants who maim and kill."

"Where did you get this information?"

"My niece got involved with the group. They took her up north to the mountains. She hasn't been herself since; she's had therapy for the atrocities they inflicted on her. They're brutal."

"What did they do to her?" My mouth felt especially dry as I struggled to grasp this conversation.

"She watched animal torture and sacrifices. She was forced to drink blood and she was raped by several of the men in the group."

"I'm sorry. I'm sorry it happened to her."

"She's failing school, can't sleep, and is losing patches of her hair. She's such a bright kid, too." He looked disgusted.

"Why Hank, then? Why do you think Hank is involved?" My questions were a whisper.

"The family hired an investigator. Hank was photographed leading the group with a woman named Jeanie. They were photographed having sex on the altar during a ritual. We have extensive photographic evidence of them performing cruel and malicious acts."

I felt weak, like I was going to pass out.

"Could I see these photographs?" I asked against my best judgment.

"The Justice Department has them right now. We're still trying to make an arrest in the case. My brother may have kept a copy of one or two photographs. Do you want me to call him?"

"Yes," I said, then "no, maybe not right now. Maybe later. I don't know what to think."

"Is he some kind of boyfriend?" Alex asked.

"He's a friend, and I care about him. I really don't want to discuss my relationship with him." My tiredness added to my confusion as my entire world upended itself.

"I'd feel better if you didn't see him," Alex said stiffly.

"He's a customer. I've been waiting on him for years."

"Let's go up north and I'll show you what we have on this guy. I want you to understand who you're dealing with."

"When? I'm awfully busy right now."

"Tonight. It just takes a few hours to get there. Then we'd be up in the mountains with the romantic moon, just you and me. We could have a great time."

"You go up north? I thought you were strictly a city guy."

"I started going there after my niece Brenda's unfortunate episode. I made a few trips and learned to appreciate the area. Want to go tonight, Stephanie?"

"No, not tonight. I'm too exhausted from working. I'll have to think about it. Maybe in a few days."

"Call me in the morning. We could go then. I'll cancel my appointments."

"I don't think so, Alex."

"Better yet, I'll spend the night here, and then I'll be here in the morning. We can decide then."

"Definitely not. I'm too exhausted—physically and emotionally. I need a good night's sleep."

"I can recharge your battery." This was Alex at his most charming and seductive.

I stood up. "Good night, my friend. I have to ask you to leave now. I'm about to either cry or scream.

He kissed me soulfully, then slipped out the front door, and headed up the street. He must have parked out of sight somewhere.

Tricksie sat in a chair, eyeing me wisely, her rust-colored eyes wide open and omniscient. She sat strangely quiet, and I appreciated her moral support in this my time of need.

"It's just you and me, Trickster. No more romance, no more men. All I need is you in my life."

* * *

Strange, disturbing dreams woke me from my sleep. Sometimes I surfaced in a panic, afraid I might be drug back under into the sleep world, sweating and confused. Most of the dreams projected dark and fearful onto the screen of my mind, but I remembered little other than my impressions.

The last dream of my fitful night seemed longest, and I walked in the woods. Lost, walking aimlessly, I felt unafraid. Trees in full leaf surrounded me, and I enjoyed the sound of the wind in the trees, leaves rustling like comforting voices. Green filled my senses, and all reflected peace and contentment.

But darkness filtered into the scene as the sun's benevolent rays sunk lower and lower. Still lost, I had no place to spend the night, and I began to feel uneasy. As the last rays of light faded away, I suddenly took hope. On a ridge high above me, a light beckoned.

The darkness covered everything, except for the light. I labored, stumbled over downed trees, got scratched by brambles until I reached a clearing. Now I made out two lights, huge bonfires on opposite sides of the clearing.

I knew what it was, but I had to go on; I couldn't return to the pitch black of the woods. I knew in my heart I didn't want to see what lay here in this clearing.

I heard shouts, and then they were before me, wearing black robes, the sleeves lined in red. I could see them clearly, though we stood in the darkness. Each took one of my arms.

Alex and Hank surrounded me.

"Come onto my altar, Stephanie. We will invoke the power of the Dark Lord, my master, and join until our energies grow strong," Hank said, his eyes glowing red.

I felt faint and the woods swirled around me.

"Stephanie, I've waited for you. I knew you would come. Come be my High Priestess. We will adore the darkness and worship together." Alex smiled, looking relaxed and confident, and I nearly went to him.

I woke up screaming, barely aware that Tricksie jumped off the bed. As I calmed myself, I heard the insistent ring of the phone for the first time, calling me back to a saner place.

Chapter 35

My dream and waking worlds merged as I struggled to answer the phone. I reached it just before the answering machine would have kicked in.

"Hello," I said, though I still felt I stood somewhere in the forest and expected brambles to brush against my arm.

I nearly slammed the phone back down when I heard Alex's voice. "Ready to go?" he said.

"Go where?" My disorientation continued.

"To the mountains, dear lady."

"I stayed there all night."

"What?"

"Never mind. I'm not awake. I have to decide this later."

"Later suits me fine. I'll give you ten minutes. That's when I'll arrive at your house." I heard the click and knew he'd hung up.

I bounded out of bed and decided instantly. Yes, I'd go to the mountains with Alex. I had to clear up this nonsense right away. It drained my energy.

I wanted my nice, old life back.

I jumped into the shower, and then dressed quickly before he got here. I was throwing clothes into a bag when the doorbell rang.

"Come in, Alex," I yelled. In two beats he was in my bedroom. "I just have to get some breakfast, and then I'll be ready."

"We can eat on the road. I haven't had breakfast, either. Just grab your things and we'll go."

Alex looked subdued this morning, pale and tired, very casual in a gray sweatshirt and black sweat pants. His black hair stuck out where it shouldn't have. He held a teal travel mug and sipped slowly at the coffee that sent delicious vapors into my room, waking me up.

He hardly looked the part of villain—more like a worn-out, unruly child.

"I have to put out the things the cat needs. We will be back tonight, won't we?"

"Don't you want to spend the night with me?"

"I have to work tomorrow. In fact, I have to start early for Rosemary." I crossed my fingers behind my back to neutralize my lie.

"I suppose so, then. Whatever you want, dear. I just want to clear things up between us."

I put out extra food and water for Tricksie, who'd hidden somewhere when Alex came in. I cleaned her litter box and washed my hands.

"You go on out. I'll be there in a minute. I've got to say goodbye to Tricksie."

He scowled, took my bag, and disappeared out the front door. I waited in the kitchen until she appeared a minute later, and I picked her up and hugged her, comforted by her soft fur.

"I'll be back tonight. Go easy on all that food, girl."

I inhaled deeply and headed out the front door, watching to make sure Tricksie didn't dart on past me.

* * *

The miles disappeared like magic, for Alex entertained me with his chatter, and soon we'd reached the familiar two-lane roads and the unpaved ones. He whipped onto a gravel road before we reached Apple Grove, a track that appeared to lead up into the mountains.

"I don't know this part of the woods," I commented and examined the pines and other trees flashing by.

"I didn't think you knew anything about this up north country," he said, glancing my way.

"Oh, I drove up here on a little trip with a friend a while ago. You know—getting back to nature, that sort of thing." Somehow, I'd never told him about Flo, Isis, and our Circle. I didn't intend to tell him now.

We drove on in silence, bobbing in our seats from the ruts and washed out spots in the road. We'd stopped several hours before for breakfast, so I wasn't hungry.

"We're almost there," he said and pulled onto a dirt road. We'd ridden nearly a half hour, but hadn't gone far. Fortunately, the day was fair, with a clear sky and mild temperatures. I couldn't imagine sliding around these roads in the rain.

The dirt road ran right up to a cabin in a small clearing. The cabin, painted bright red, looked small, but well-kept, with mountain laurel bushes in front.

"Here we are!" Alex said as he got out of his Cadillac.

"Where are we? What is this?" I asked, mystified as to what he was showing me.

"It's their hideout, the demonic cult people. Didn't I tell you I'd expose Hank and his followers? This is their base of operations here in the mountains."

"How do you know that?" I felt caution in the air.

"The investigator found it for us. He was great at tracking them down. He even figured out how to get in the building."

Alex walked around the back of the cottage and came back with a key. "I just put everything back when I'm done. I've never been caught in the act." He leaned down to unlock the front door.

"This is breaking and entering. It's against the law. We should get out of here." Caution became concern and disbelief.

He smiled benevolently at me.

"You want to find out about the cult members, don't you? Sometimes the end justifies the means. We're not dealing with a group who gives a hoot about the law. They make up their own law as they grope in the darkness. Do you think I care at all about their rights? I'd say they've given up their rights by their gruesome actions on others." He opened the front door wide.

"What if one of them comes?" I asked as my final plea.

"They usually come at night. We'll be fine, Steph. Trust me."

I saw artifacts everywhere; my mouth hung open in shock, for I hadn't expected immediate confirmation of Alex's claims.

Above the fireplace hung an upside down crucifix, and on the mantel sat skulls of various sizes and shapes. One of them looked human. Black robes hung from hooks on the walls. On end tables on either side of an aged couch sat carved phalluses, large and wooden, the wood aged and dark.

"There's more in the bedrooms," Alex said.

"I don't think I want to see any more. I've seen quite enough. You've proved the cult uses this cottage."

"I can show you some sites out on the mountain, not just the one uncovered by the Boy Scouts," he said, pointing with one outstretched arm.

It was obvious, really. Alex knew where all the sites were, but that didn't prove Hank was involved. If anything, it pointed to Alex's involvement. I wasn't sure what to do.

"You feel faint?" Alex stared at me. "You've gotten very quiet all of a sudden."

"How does Hank fit into all this? You've said he's the cult leader, but none of this proves that. What can you show me that connects him with this group?"

"I thought just showing you this would convince you. I should have called my brother about those pictures. Steph, don't you believe in me? I thought we were best buddies."

I thought of Hank and the years I had known him versus the few months I had known Alex.

"I guess it has to be one of you. You claim it's Hank. Hank claims it's you. I'd be glad if a third party showed up and took the rap."

"I'm not understanding your attitude." He sounded hurt.

"Let's get something to eat. I just had a bagel before, and we haven't had lunch yet. All this detective work makes a woman hungry."

My stomach was balled in knots by the time we reached the diner and were shown to a seat by the windows.

"I have to make a few calls. I'll just stop outside for a few minutes," Alex said after we ordered. He wielded his cell phone.

I waved him on and grabbed my back pack, rummaging through its contents. I took my busy bag with me whenever I thought I might have an idle moment. I thought about grabbing a mystery novel I'd not successfully gotten into yet, but then my hands grasped the black volume with white lettering. I'd forgotten it was in the bag.

Flo's Book of Shadows.

I flipped through the pages, waiting for something to jump out at me, some dark secret. Instead, I saw colorful flowers she'd drawn in purple, red, and green inks. Her flower art circled a recipe for mulled cider. The ingredients sounded tasty, with spices added to cider and heated up. I scanned the directions and suddenly stopped as though I'd spied a poisonous coral snake on my leg.

At the very bottom of the directions, slipped in between parentheses was the following: (H. Priest—412-555-0111).

I sat frozen in my seat as the sweat broke out, dizziness descending on me in waves.

It was Alex's cell phone number.

Chapter 36

In my earlier dream, Kwan Yin said part of me knew who the cult leader was. After the shock passed away, that knowing engaged. Yes, I had known for some time that Alex was the guilty party. That knowledge lay just beneath the surface. Now it all seemed so obvious.

I looked around the diner. Alex must still be outside with his cell phone, and I knew what I had to do.

Kim was working tonight, the waitress who had sent her brother to escort Isis and me in the woods. I sighed in relief. I enjoyed seeing a friendly face again. She was working on the other side of the diner, so I walked over as she cleaned up a table.

"Kim," I said, "it's good to see you again."

"I remember you. You came in with another woman and wanted to visit where that poor woman burned up."

"Your brother helped us tremendously. Listen, I need to make an important phone call, and I can't use the pay phone because my friend might overhear what I'm saying. I feel like I might be in danger. It's related to the murder of that woman. Is there a phone in the back I could use?" I flashed my calling card at her startled face.

"Sure," she said, "I want to help you. Should I call the police?"

"It's too soon for that. I have to call a private investigator on the case. I need to hurry before he comes back in."

She whisked me into the back, where a touch tone phone hung on the wall. I quickly punched in the calling card numbers and then Hank's phone number and waited as each ring took an eternity.

He answered.

"Hank, this is Stephanie. I have something for you that might help the investigation."

"Where are you, Steph? What's going on? I've been trying to reach you."

"I came up to Apple Grove with Alex. He wanted to prove to me that you were the High Priest. All he did was show me a cabin where they keep their stuff. He didn't really have evidence of your involvement, not that I thought you were implicated." I hoped Hank didn't think I'd ever suspected him, though I had.

"What are you doing now? Are you in danger? Should I come up there?"

"We're eating at the diner. I don't think I'm in danger, and I think we'll be leaving to come home soon. No need for you to make the trip.

"But I have to tell you why I called. We have a journal Flo Pohaski kept, and I stumbled across something in it tonight. She wrote down 'H. Priest' and a phone number. It's Alex's cell phone number."

"Nice going. That sounds like solid evidence. We'll nail this guy before you know it."

"I've got to go. I don't want him to get suspicious."

"Take care. Be mighty careful around him. I'll check my messages frequently in case you need to call me again. Can you call me when you get home?" I heard the concern in his voice.

"It might be late, Hank."

"Call me. I'll go back to sleep. Just call me."

"I will."

I hung up, feeling reassured, and hurried out to the diner. Alex sat at our table, a smile fixed on his face.

"Where were you?" he asked.

"Everybody has their phone calls to make. I just don't have a cell phone. Some of us are underprivileged."

"What about the pay phone?" He motioned to the one on the diner wall. I began to feel uneasy about all the questions.

"Someone else was using it. Besides, it's too noisy in here. I needed to call my neighbor to check the cat. He checks on her when I'm gone."

Our waitress brought the food, a tantalizing diversion from talk of phone calls. We ate quickly, in silence. For once, we had nothing to say to each other.

"I forgot something at the cabin," Alex blurted out. I raised my eyebrows.

"My watch is missing. I took it off behind the cabin when I was fishing for the key and forgot about it. I can't leave it there. The deviants might find me out and come after me. That Hank guy might sic the devil and assorted demons on me." He made a weird face, and I couldn't help but laugh.

"Oh Alex, I was hoping to get home and relax a little on my day off. You're spoiling all my plans."

He grinned, and I saw a glimmer in his eyes. "I've spoiled many a plan before."

"All right, then. Let's retrieve your watch. The sooner done, the better. I believe you."

We'd driven nearly back to the cabin when I wished I was home, a sudden pang of longing for Tricksie and the comforts of my little house. I settled back and told myself I'd be there soon, aware of Alex's presence. Even though I had evidence he was the cult leader, it hadn't sunken in yet. He was still Alex to me.

Finally, we pulled in before the red cabin, and Alex jumped out, pocketing the SUV keys. "I'll just be a minute," he said with a wink.

I waited, listening to birds of the forest. I waited until I knew it was taking too long. "Alex," I called through the Cadillac's open window.

No answer. I got out and gently latched the door, knowing something was wrong. I steered myself around the side of the cabin until I stopped in my tracks.

No Alex. I called softly to him and examined the back of the cabin, which abutted the pine trees. I saw a back door, but no signs of life anywhere.

I began to feel panic, so I walked around front and banged on the door. I was yelling his name when the door opened with a creak.

He stood there wearing a black robe with a red sash, an eager smile on his face.

"What's going on, Alex? How did you get in there?"

"I do have a key to the back door. I was hoping to lure you into the cabin. See how it worked?" he said, drawing me in beside him. He tried to kiss me, but I resisted, disliking his trickery. I felt uneasy and suddenly on edge.

"What's wrong, Stephanie? Having second thoughts about me?" His words mocked me.

"You aren't who you say you are. There's an entire part of you I don't know anything about."

"So you think I'm the leader of the cult, is that it? You think your friend Hank is innocent."

"I think you're the High Priest. I have evidence to prove it, although it all seems insane. I can't imagine why you would get involved in such cruelty."

"I've lost you, haven't I?" He held my face in his hands. "Not again. I can't bear to lose you again."

"Again?" I said, yet a dream flickered in my brain, the one with flames, Flo who wasn't Flo, and the tall, dark figure—a dream I'd had weeks ago.

He stared into my eyes.

"You do remember, don't you, my love?"

"I don't. Not at all. Sometimes I see a tiny piece of it in a dream, but I don't remember. I don't know what you're taking about."

"Think about it, my dear, and it'll all come back to you as it has to me." He led me into one of the bedrooms and then left, slamming the door. I heard the key turning as he locked the door behind him.

"Where are you going?" I screamed through the door as I pounded on it.

"I'll be back."

"I want to go home. I have to get back tonight," I screamed, but I could hear him close the front door, and I knew I was trapped.

No one knew where I was, only Alex.

Alex, the High Priest.

* * *

First I'd searched for a way out of the bedroom. Its one window with the shade pulled wouldn't budge, locked tight from the outside. Black candles, phallic objects, and a disturbing painting hanging across from the bed depicting Lucifer and the fallen in a bloody orgy—none of it helped allay my fears. I schemed to break out until I crumpled onto the bed in exasperation and fell asleep.

How long I slept, I don't know, but I awoke suddenly (had I heard a sound?) and it had gone dark outside. Or was it the dream that had wakened me? I'd dreamed of the fires again.

This time Alex was being held back by two men and I was being led away. I could hear him screaming and struggling to loosen himself.

"Come back, my love. I'm so sorry. It was all a mistake," he cried.

Then there were flames and I congregated with my friends, mostly maidens like myself. We were all being led away and tied to wooden stakes. A crowd surrounded us, and I could see the old woman who was Flo laughing and tossing her head. She looked delighted.

I longed to stretch out my arms to him, my man who was crying into his hands, but I couldn't move. Finally, they led him away, and the fires were lit and a lusty crackling of fire filled our town square.

I awoke smelling the flames, but also knowing more than before. Yes, Flo was the woman who turned us in, we witches practicing gently in the forest. Flo turned us in to an authority, she'd said in her journal.

Suddenly, I realized who the authority had been. I almost had all the pieces of the puzzle.

I heard the front door pulled open, then the key in the bedroom lock. I waited on the bed as my lover of old returned to me. I now looked forward to the final installment of the story.

"You in there, Stephie?" I heard him say when the bedroom door had opened. I hadn't even noticed the darkness, as it blended in so with my dream.

His speech was slow and slurred, and I heard him stumbling in the darkness.

"I need to know the rest of the story of long ago. I know most of it now," I said.

He stopped. "What story?"

"The witches from the forest who were turned in by Flo in a past life to a man in authority—long, long ago. That man caused his love to be burned at the stake. I think those lovers were you and me, Alex. I just don't know what happened."

"Oh, I'll talk, Stephie. I'll tell you everything." He reached me and swung me up into his unsteady arms. "But first we have a ritual to the Dark Lord to attend. Come on out here and look."

He carried me outdoors where the moon still looked full, nearly blazing with light.

"Great night for a ritual, ain't it, Steph?"

Chapter 37

Alex deposited me like a bag of groceries on the front seat of the Cadillac vehicle. I waited as he got in, wondering if I was being foolish for not trying to run.

But where was there to run to? We were on a deserted mountain, with no other cars or buildings in sight. Should I blindly strike out into the dark?

He drove us further up the mountain, his steering precise and cool. If I didn't know better, I'd think he wasn't drunk.

"Why did you turn me in? Why did you turn in me and the other witches in that other lifetime?"

"Who told you that?" he asked sharply.

"I dreamed it. Just now, while you were gone. Besides, Flo Pohaski told us she'd turned us in during a past lifetime to an authority. She said she'd been responsible for our untimely deaths back then."

"You knew that wretched woman? I've never met a more miserable soul."

"I belonged to the same women's group. She got insulted one day and left us, claiming she'd joined a much more powerful group. How did you know her, Alex?"

"She joined our group. From the first moment I met her, old memories were triggered. Dreams and waking visions told me the story.

"I was clergy in that long ago time, the Burning Times. You were my much loved wife, and I cherished you. Flo came to me, denouncing witches who met in the woods, dancing by candlelight, worshipping the old gods.

"Flo knew you were one of the witches, yet I didn't. You'd secretly joined them, and much to my horror, when the witches were seized one full moon, you were among them. Imagine my horror, Stephanie, my agony, when I discovered you among those taken. For I could not save you—the deed was done and they burned you at the stake.

"So you see, my dear, when I discovered who the Flo woman was, I had no choice. For I am no longer some religious person, not even the atheist I have been for so long.

"I've sold my soul to the devil, and you and I haven't a chance in hell to be happy together."

I tried to watch our route, but he'd made multiple turns, and I was already lost, a lost little babe in the woods. His words moved me, but I knew that lifetime occurred hundreds of years in the past.

Here and now were all that mattered.

He turned onto a road that ended abruptly in the woods, then parked at its end. "This way to the party," he said, jumping out and opening my door.

"I don't want to do this, Alex," I said, not moving.

"It'll be good for you, my dear," he said and hauled me out.

He'd grabbed a lantern from somewhere, shining it forward, onto a path in the woods. I went along ahead of him, so he could keep an eye on me, he said. The night felt mellow, as the moon cast a silvery coating on everything.

We walked forever, and through emotional drain laced with terror, I'd grown quite tired. Just as I thought I couldn't plod another step, Alex came up to me and took me by my arm.

We'd reached a small clearing, and there were signs the site had been used. Alex cast his lantern light around, revealing old fires and a wooden altar.

"Nobody home, Stephie. Just the way I like it. Just you, me, and some demons."

"Why have you brought me here? Whatever can you be planning?" I felt sweat on my brow unrelated to any exertion.

"The worship of Satan and the darkness is very important to me and the power is strong tonight with this moon. You ought to know that."

"But my circle of women friends believes there is no Satan. We believe in the God and Goddess. Satan doesn't even exist." I hadn't meant to, but my voice had become loud, insistent.

He turned to me, and I could see his features in the moonlight. "You and I never have believed in the same things, have we? But we always did believe in each other."

He wrapped his arms around me, and for an instant I relaxed into him. He lifted me, placed me upon the altar and had me tied to it before I knew what he was doing.

"You're very good at tying things up," I said. The world seemed dreamy and unreal, and he had me trussed before I could resist.

"My dark lord requires it of me. And how dare you question the mighty power of the devil. Who are you to deny his existence? That's blasphemy!"

"The dark side consists more of our own fears and ignorance, greed, lust—that sort of thing. Our shadow self. Our ego. Satan was fashioned after the pagan horned god, who is loving and life-giving."

"You're going to make an atheist of me again if I keep listening to you. You're damned confusing to a poor lost child like me."

"Seriously," I said, feeling like a shish kebob tied on a stick from my altar spot, "can you tell me why you did it? Why did you get involved in all this demonic bullshit? Why did you hurt all those creatures and burn old flaky Flo?"

"Flo was a different story. I told you—she ruined my life once upon a time. As for the rest, I think I was bored. I could have sex with any woman I wanted, I was making plenty of money in business. It was just all so easy and boring. I needed excitement to add meaning to my life. And then Alice stumbled upon this devil worship thing. She's really into it, and it made her passionate again."

He stared softly into the darkness beyond me.

"Maybe that's not it, Steph. Maybe the whole cult and ritual detour was so that you and I would be together again. It has been great to be with you. In fact, the way I feel when I'm with you is a hundred times better than the devil bullshit, as you call it. I haven't felt this way since I was a kid."

"So what are you going to do with me?" I asked.

"I don't even know, dear. I could sacrifice you on this altar, but I love you. Of course, I could get big brownie points with Satan for a juicy morsel like you." The moonlight revealed a black-handled knife with a long, silver blade in his right hand.

"There is no Satan. You'd be wasting your energy," I said, feeling tiny prickles of fear along my arms and legs.

He held the knife's blade against my neck, and I strained to get away from it.

"But what if you're wrong?" he said.

I could feel the metal pressing into my flesh, and I screamed and screamed until he clamped a hand over my mouth.

"Quiet, Stephie, quiet. No need to scare away the hooty owls and squirrels. I was just killing you, I mean kidding you. I think the booze makes me stupid. I did most of my ritual work under the influence."

He stood up tall, clearing his throat and releasing my mouth.

"Time for me to go, sweetie. I guess I won't ever see you again."

"Where are you going?"

"Got to get out of Pittsburgh. They'll track me down and I might get hurt. I don't feel safe here anymore."

"I turned you in," I said softly to him. "I have evidence you're the leader. I guess karma has gotten back to us; you turned me in, then I turned you in."

He looked dumbstruck, as if he was going to cry.

"How could you do that? I thought we were buddies. We were lovers."

He seized me, holding me as tightly as he could in my tied-down position. We kissed passionately, and then he stood up and stared at me.

"There are islands all over the oceans—in the Mediterranean, the South Pacific. Plenty of places to slip away to and hide. I could take you with me. We'd have a great life together."

His words stirred me on some level, but I wasn't even tempted. I knew who I was, something he had yet to learn.

"Goodbye, Alex. I hope you hide away safely. I hope you find plenty of joy and adventure. I'm staying here, love."

He nodded his head and stared intently at me. For nearly a minute, I saw him, the man from my vision, his face superimposed on Alex's. Again, the eyes of love, tender and infinite, transcending time and space, gazed at me from Alex's face. I lay still on the hard wood altar, mesmerized, until he moved away, and the spell was broken.

He waved a farewell, turned, and headed across the clearing. "Maybe I'll reform, stop my ugly ways. Maybe we'll be together in the next lifetime," he called.

"Alex!" I screamed. "Don't leave me here!"

He shrugged his shoulders in the moonlight, and disappeared into the woods.

I shivered in my light clothing; the night had grown chilly. I heard noises far off, scrambling sounds, then screeching sounds even nearer. I shivered again, telling myself not to be afraid. Yet my situation became more chillingly clear with each passing minute.

I was beyond the middle of nowhere. No one knew I was here. I was tied up and couldn't escape this altar with no food or water, exposed to the elements and forest creatures.

I thought about my studies and roots as a witch.

"I call upon the nature spirits and angels of this forest. I need help. Please assist me in whatever way you can," I called out passionately, but with no hysteria. I knew my prayer would be answered. "Thank you for your help, angels and little fairies."

Time flowed by. It could have been a half hour or even an hour later when I began to wonder if there were bears in this forest. I was thinking there were, when I caught movement from the side of my eye.

I held my breath a full minute.

He was beautiful in the moonlight, every silvery-gray hair pronounced, his ears pointed upright, his coat full and regal. He gazed at me steadfastly with chilling yellow eyes that could see the world beyond this one.

He looked so beautiful and other-worldly that I forgot to be afraid, not even now as he padded toward me, this ghost of the night.

"Hello, brother wolf," I whispered.

Chapter 38

I closed my eyes as he drew near, felt his warm breath on my cheek, then a gentle lick on my face. When I opened my eyes, he had gone.

Only moments later, I heard shouts, heard my name called. Looking around, I saw Ralph and Kim. They both untied me, and Ralph helped me, with my cramped, aching limbs, down from the altar.

"You two are like a vision from heaven. I had no idea how I was going to get out of this one. How did you end up here?"

"Part mountain ingenuity, part pure luck. Your friend Hank called me at the station," Ralph the mechanic said.

"Does Hank know you?" I asked in amazement.

"We know each other from his trips up here investigating the cult, the murder of Ms. Pohaski. So he called me a few hours ago, asking questions. I'd seen you ride past in the black Cadillac SUV—anyway, it looked like you. I trotted down to the diner, and Kim said you'd been there. Her description of the man with you matched that of the High Priest that Hank gave me.

"Hank was awfully worried you were in trouble. He said you'd called him, said you were here, that you'd be home soon. Then you didn't come home. He said he had a strong feeling you were in trouble. He asked me to find you and do whatever necessary. I'd really hoped to grab this Alex guy and give him some demonic pats on the back. What happened to him?"

"He took off. Just left me here," I said vaguely.

"Where did he go?" Kim asked.

"I don't really know. Said something about a place out west." I was amazed to hear myself covering for him. *Run, Alex,* I thought, *run fast and far.*

"Did he hurt you?" Ralph asked.

I smiled at him. "He just scared me. There were a few anxious moments, that was all. The worst was when he left me trussed to the altar. I didn't expect anyone to find me. How did you find me, anyway?"

"It wasn't as easy as it looked. We've been searching for hours. I knew of a couple ritual sites on the mountain—the one where Flo Pohaski was killed and one other, but not this one. I tried to find the cabin you'd told Hank about, but no luck. We were actually headed back to the diner when we saw the wolf," Ralph said.

"You saw the wolf?" I said, incredulous. He now seemed like a dream.

"He crossed right in front of us on the road, big gray fellow. Stared right at us. I had to stop so I wouldn't hit him. Then he just stood at the side of the road, looking at me."

"It was my idea to track him. It looked like he wanted us to follow him," Kim said.

"He took us to a track, then a path, then we lost him, but we heard his howl and sometimes glimpsed his tail till we found this place. I don't know how we would have found you otherwise. Did you see him, too?" Ralph asked.

"He licked my cheek, then disappeared. I thought I dreamed him."

"Maybe we all dreamed him, Stephanie. Lucky dream for you," Kim said.

"Let's get back to the diner. You must be hungry, and Hank should be there by now. That's what we were doing when the wolf appeared—going to meet Hank," Ralph said.

Hank. Hank had come. Any fears of intimacy were crowded out by relief and gratitude. I needed comfort now and someone to trust.

"You're awfully lucky he came up here," Ralph said as we trudged through the woods. I felt like I'd been stomping through woods all my life. Ralph's flashlight cut a cheerful beam through the trees.

"Oh, I know that, Ralph. Any reason in particular you say that?" I asked.

"For one thing, how were you going to get home? Your ride left without you."

"That's right. I hadn't thought of that. He left me tied up in the middle of nowhere without transportation. I guess I'm not speaking to him anymore," I said, thinking, *Run, Alex, run.* Something about my connection with him in that past life made me root for him, strange as that may seem. Part of me still clung to him in another realm of reality where he had been a loving husband.

"I think you're a lucky woman," Ralph said.

He drove us through the darkness to the diner. When I saw Hank's Bronco, I felt a wave of relief wash over me. Someone who loved me had come to watch over me. Someone with strength and positive intent who would drive me home.

He sat alone, drinking coffee.

"They found you. I've been worried and feeling helpless," Hank said and stood up and walked to meet me.

We embraced shamelessly before Ralph, Kim, and the other diner customers. My insecurities had vanished, as if they'd gotten lost in the forest and couldn't find their way back to me.

"He didn't hurt you, did he?" Hank asked into my hair.

"Just my pride, dear. It would have been more than that if Ralph and Kim hadn't found me. Thank you for calling Ralph." I silently thanked the Goddess and nature spirits for helping me by sending the wolf. I knew my thanks would continue over the coming days, weeks, and months.

"I just wish I could have been here sooner. I nearly lost my mind on the trip up here. I couldn't get here fast enough."

I felt full of love and joy, the despair of this day dissipating like a heavy fog lifting. I said one last quick prayer for Alex that he would escape and harm no one again. The universe would have to take care of him now.

"I just have one question for you," I said, looking into Hank's incredible green eyes.

"What's that, Stephanie?"

"Can I get you a piece of cherry pie to go with your coffee?"

* * *

A perfect blue sky complemented the sun's artistry, for every blade of grass, every flower and ribbon glistened with energy. We'd gathered here at South Park atop this hill in the woods in an isolated section of the park. The trees were beginning to bud, the ground growing warmer as spring thawed our recollections of winter. This May 1st, Beltane, we stood in a circle around the Maypole, dressed in our finery.

Spring winds tugged at the long, pink dress with the red and purple flowers I wore. Beside me, Hank's cotton shirt matched his fabulous green eyes. He wore khaki pants at this, his first ritual with me.

Many of the women wore long dresses or outfits with long skirts, yet some dressed in casual tops and slacks. The men alternated ordinary street dress with special ritual wear with shirts with baggy long sleeves, vests, and rough-hewn pants.

"What's the idea behind this Maypole?" Hank asked. We still waited for the event to begin, but even the waiting felt pleasant and festive.

"I still have a lot to learn about these holidays and rituals. But I do know the Maypole is a phallic symbol, the weaving of the ribbons around it symbolizes the female genitalia. Beltane's all about fertility. Coupling."

Hank raised his eyebrows, and I admired our Maypole. It stood about eight feet tall, a metal pole with flowers attached to its top, colorful long ribbons being teased by the breeze. I took a long, full inhale of the delightful spring air.

"Are you going to introduce me to your friend?" a voice said into my left ear.

I turned and hugged Isis, who looked gorgeous as ever in her purple flowered halter top with purple chiffon skirt. She wore flowers in her hair, long, gold chains with gemstones around her neck.

"You haven't met Hank?" I asked.

She solemnly shook her head, though her eyes were merry.

"This is Hank Shepherd, and this is Isis. Deborah Woodman is her original name. I didn't realize you hadn't met each other."

"So you helped solve the mystery of Flo Pohaski's murder," Hank said to Isis.

"I tried, but it was Stephanie who came up with all the really great stuff."

"Yes, but you were the mastermind, Isis. You got us involved in the first place." Isis squinted a little in the sun as I spoke.

"There are a few things I'm still unclear about. Just this morning, I remembered your neighbor Tony with the cross in his attic who made trips up to the forest. What was that all about?"

I laughed. "I finally got the nerve to ask him about that. He was in a passion play for his church. He built the cross for that and stowed it up there in case they needed it again. So it's a religious artifact of sorts. I explained to him my real reason for snooping, but I think he was insulted all the same."

"And where is he now, this Alex guy? Has he been tracked down?" she asked.

"We're still searching for him, Isis. But we got his lady friend and other cult members who perpetrated the crimes. The group's dissolved. The high priestess doesn't think so, but somebody turned them in. I think it was our missing Alex. Someone so difficult to track down in the first place probably knows how to vanish and reappear in a new location," Hank said.

"You helped track him, didn't you, Hank?" Isis said.

"I did many hours of investigating, but came up with little evidence. Even his license plate was traced to a stolen vehicle. Stephanie made all the real breaks in the case.

"But I've forgotten to ask you one detail that bothers me. Where was Flo after she disappeared from here, after she quit her job?"

Isis answered eagerly. "We don't have all the answers yet. We're guessing Flo lived with cult people up north. We did trace her through a few social work jobs she applied for and didn't get in Clarion. In addition, the mail deliveries at her home here were held at the post office and she picked them up every two weeks. After the beginning of December, she no longer made the pickups."

"So we think she died around the middle of December from that fact and her journal entries. Isis got a note from her in January, but we later deciphered the postmark to be early December," I added.

"She was a foolish woman, her death needless," Hank said.

Isis and I locked meaningful gazes.

"I agree, but karma weighed heavily against her," Isis said.

Our leader for the ritual motioned and started talking, and Isis moved to her spot in the circle. Hank reached for my hand and gave it a squeeze.

"We need less talk about Flo and more about important subjects," he said in a subdued tone.

"Such as?"

"I think I'm going to like Beltane," he whispered in my ear.

I couldn't stop the big smile that blossomed on my face.

"Me, too, Hank. Beltane never looked better."

The End

AND IF YOU ENJOYED READING THIS BOOK, PLEASE LEAVE A REVIEW ON AMAZON, telling what you enjoyed about it. Your review will help others find my books. Thanks so much!

DON'T FORGET your FREE BOOK, *Tales of the Wild & Seldom Seen.* It's a gift for joining Cathy's email list (to learn about upcoming releases, walking between the worlds, other realms, and free stuff).

Sign up at **www.CathyACorn.com.**

THE FAERIES ARE HERE TO MAKE YOUR DREAMS COME TRUE!

BLUE MOON OVER MADAGASCAR
Lilith and the Faeries Series #1

Pittsburgh bookstore manager Lilith Devlin meets a faery in her garden, who asks her to write a book explaining faery ways and to tackle a special mission. In exchange, the wee one promises romance and adventure.

Though Lilith fears change, she soon travels to Ireland to learn from the fae, meets an attractive New York editor, and flies to Madagascar with him to stop poachers from destroying endangered lemurs. Her world expands in unexpected ways as she grows closer to the faeries and discovers the mysteries of nature …and love.

Available at Amazon for 99 cents (usually).

WAIT, THERE'S MORE!

SMELL THE PLUMERIAS
Lilith and the Faeries Series #2

Lilith and new love Adam relax on the Big Island of Hawaii, a "free" vacation from the faeries, until a beloved dolphin friend is murdered. As they investigate this tragedy, they unveil an even more disturbing mystery: who is invoking the wrath of Pele, volcano goddess?

Amidst increasing volcanic eruptions, earthquake tremors, and threat of tsunamis, they race to solve these puzzles as they seek to grow closer to nature, this island paradise, the faeries, and each other.

Available at Amazon.

A TEST OF THEIR LOVE FOR EACH OTHER

FAERY: THE FINAL FRONTIER
Lilith and the Faeries Series #3

The faeries contact Lilith and Adam about the Dream People, a tribe in a remote, mountainous region of the Ecuadorian rain forest. The tribe meditates to heal the world, and nearby oil drilling threatens their mission.

Lilith, Adam, and four shamans explore the forest to find the one man responsible. As a further challenge, Lilith and Adam's love must be tested to solve the mystery.

Available at Amazon.

CAN SHE SAVE HERSELF?

MURDER THROUGH THE LOOKING-GLASS

Psychotherapist Suzanne Westin counsels clients about relationship problems, but she's a failure at romance, contenting herself with her puppy and newly acquired Victorian near Pittsburgh.

Yet the crystal ball she buys and gazes into reveals an intriguing scenario—a past life in this same house as a blonde singer with a 1940's swing band. An even more disturbing vision shows her past self lying dead in the woods, and she learns she must solve the mystery or history will repeat itself—soon—in this paranormal mystery & suspense novel.

Available at Amazon.

Acknowledgements

There's a lot of misunderstanding about who witches, or those belonging to the Wiccan religion, traditionally were, and how they operated in antiquity. They were the healers, gathering herbs and tending to the sick. They lived close to the earth, in tune with Mother Earth and her cycles. The only power they had was of love—in listening to nature and heeding her call. Like other shamans, they usually walked between the worlds of what we call ordinary reality and the spirit world.

Throughout history, they were persecuted and killed, as many other humans have been in other lands and for other reasons. Those were and still are the dark times. Letting in more light was always their calling, and even today, Wiccans perform ceremonies to raise the energy to heal themselves and the planet.

I was fortunate enough to attend rituals in Pittsburgh, to get a taste of what being a Wiccan might involve. I am grateful to those groups for welcoming me, for my dear friend Barbara and her leadership, and for the pagan groups that still perform ceremony. My fascination with shamanism may be in part to a connection with things Wiccan in another dimension of reality.

I am grateful to all those who treasure this earth and the natural world. Such reverence is not only commendable, but necessary, since the world's health is at stake here. Treating the environment with a cavalier attitude is no longer an option, for if we destroy our home, we cannot build another.

Just as there are those who would wreck this beautiful planet and leave the mess behind, there are lightworkers here who continue to call in the light.

I believe in love and light, and that even the smallest spark will illuminate the darkness and make us whole again. I rejoice that there are those who connect deeply with the natural world and hear her messages. There's great joy in the undertaking. I hope you'll include this in your own journey, your walk on the earth in this lifetime.

There's really nothing else like it.

And don't forget to go outside and sing to the faeries. They enjoy that sort of thing.

Namaste.

ABOUT THE AUTHOR

Cathy A. Corn, RN, RM, LMT, lives happily-ever-after in Pittsburgh with husband Alan and critters Cato and Cleo. She practices massage/energy work and speaks and teaches about the faeries. Her study of healing spans many years and still fascinates her more than dusting furniture.

Learn more and sign up for her mailing list to receive a free book or novella at **www.CathyACorn.com,** where she blogs about healers, healing, and the wonders of the natural world. You can also touch base with her on her Facebook page, Cathy A. Corn, Author. She believes your dreams can come true—don't you?

And don't forget to go outside and visit the faeries.

www.ingramcontent.com/pod-product-compliance
Lightning Source LLC
LaVergne TN
LVHW091113080826
845145LV00008B/1892

* 9 7 8 1 7 3 3 3 2 1 6 1 7 *